Curse of the Tomb Seekers

A Zimbell House Anthology

Curse of the Tomb Seekers

A Zimbell House Anthology

This book is a work of fiction. Any references to historical events, real people, or real locales are used fictitiously. All characters appearing in this work are the product of the individual author's imagination, and any resemblance to actual persons, living or dead is entirely coincidental.

All rights reserved, including the right of reproduction in whole or in part in any form. No part of this publication may be reproduced, distributed, or transmitted in any form or by any means, including photocopying, recording, or other electronic or mechanical methods, without the written permission of the publisher.

For permission requests, write to the publisher at the address below:
Attention: Permissions Coordinator
Zimbell House Publishing, LLC
PO Box 1172
Union Lake, Michigan 48387
mailto: info@zimbellhousepublishing.com

© 2015 Zimbell House Publishing, LLC
Cover Design by The Book Planners
www.TheBookPlanners.com

Published in the United States by Zimbell House Publishing LLC
http://www.ZimbellHousePublishing.com
All Rights Reserved

Print ISBN: 978—942818-45-8
Kindle ISBN: 978-1-942818-46-5
Digital ISBN: 978-1-942818-53-3
Trade Paper ISBN: 978-1-945967-46-7
Library of Congress Control Number: 2015917493

First Edition: November/2015
10 9 8 7 6 5 4

Acknowledgements

Zimbell House Publishing would like to thank all the writers that submitted to our anthology. We chose eight contributors that we felt best represented the spirit of *Curse of the Tomb Seekers*.

We would also like to thank all those on our Zimbell House team whose hard work made this project worthwhile.

A special thanks to The Book Planners for the cover design.

Contents

Cursed Blood

Matthew Wilson

Scotland 1950

"Open! If you have any charity, then please open up."

Thunder lit the figure of the old house as he opened the door, a walking stick jabbed out as if he were blind, but his eyes caught all the fire of thunder in the angry sky. "What the hell do you want, son?"

"Sanctuary, please," Richard sobbed. "My car broke down along the lane and I beg a bed for the night."

The old man scowled, peering behind the strangers sodden shoulders as if expecting some trick, that this bold youth was a scouting party wishing to know how many marbles the owner retained when the others came and attacked. Finally, the old man recognized no danger and stepped aside.

Richard dived in through the door before the old man changed his mind and headed for the radiators. "Thank you, I am Richard."

"I care not, keep the rain for yourself; get none on my wallpaper."

What a grouch, Richard thought and removed his coat with care, expecting great columns of steam to rise off him as he moved into the living room–the heat buzzing from the throbbing radiators was glorious.

"I am sorry to trouble you," Richard said, his mom had brought him up to have manners, even towards those who lacked them.

"I have saved you from the storm as one more argument for my passage into heaven…by morning, I shall be no more."

Richard had trouble swallowing, *so that was certain then–this fellow was insane.* How many other travelers had come here seeking sanctuary and been murdered for their pennies? Would the old man be insulted if Richard walked out? Would he scream like an insulted wild man and run him through with that walking stick like a knight would mythical creatures?

"I've been meaning to confess for some time now," the old man noted, moving across the room and planted himself in his favorite chair from which fear had kept him prisoner for years. "Keep your rent; if you're to sleep beneath my roof tonight, then you can pay me by listening to my complaints."

The old man showed his years as exhaustion set in and he withered in the chair like a flower too long in the sun. "Sit, son and you will have a story of curses. Do you believe in evil?"

Richard looked at a bottle of brandy on the table and thought it preferable to pneumonia; it was hard now to believe this ruined man was capable of anything beyond words. "I know how to keep back its cold fangs," Richard said and asked for a drink.

The old man complied and followed suit. "A double then before I die."

Egypt 1922

Arnold disliked the heat, but after all his boasting that he could lead the expedition and the shameful letters he had sent home begging mom for money; he couldn't give up now. Since dad blew out his brains over bad business deals, Arnold had always had problems with money, but he'd struck lucky now by way of an old college friend that was heading out to Egypt on her honeymoon.

It didn't matter that she had chosen Benjamin over him, those days were over and Arnold needed money to live, not love. Attracted by the romance of ancient queens, Benjamin had been easily talked into taking Arnold along for a little digging.

Julia was against the idea, having found the letters that Arnold left at her home creepy, but she liked to make Benjamin happy and was pleased to have him all night while he worked all day in the sand.

The tomb had been discovered and all its ancient weaponry cataloged. Fools supposed that curses lay inside–a monster covered in bandages would throttle any thieves who dared intrude upon its sleeping master, but Arnold didn't believe in fairy tales–he believed in money. Now that he had enough for a home, he could move away from his mom, out from under her thumb.

All the wonderful possibilities that had been deprived of father now lay promising before Arnold. He could have fast cars and fast women...for a year. He had gone over the calculations twice and realized that if only he had the sole rights to the tomb, then he could buy a castle somewhere in the beauty of Scotland–a heavenly dream of his from childhood–if only some curses were true.

If Benjamin would be a Samaritan and reject his claim. What did he want with more money now he was so privileged as to have a wealthy father who paid for every little thing, who had never let his favorite boy starve? Who had taken the woman of Arnold's heart for himself?

The argument happened at night. Benjamin had been drinking to celebrate the dig. His name would go down in history now he had enough to build a nest egg for his wife; there was great shame on any man who inherited money. Benjamin had been here only a fortnight and had ensured his future.

"I want you to throw your contract in the fire, if you have any love for me, then you would do it," Arnold said too quickly. Benjamin was not yet drunk enough and laughed in his friends face. Benjamin had fancy lawyers, this was a man who had never starved, and who had never worked a day or suffered sickness and Arnold hated him for it.

It has to be now, he thought, as Benjamin stood with great difficulty.

"I may be drunk, sir, but I can still work a phone to keep my claim–"

Benjamin fell as Arnold picked up the fire poker and cracked him on his head. For a moment, it seemed a nightmare, an awful fertile image that Arnold's eyes had constructed through lack of sleep, but no matter how many times he blinked them, Arnold's eyes projected the same information.

Benjamin was dead, and his murderer would hang.

Even with his money worries, Arnold had lived so long through quick thinking, desperate men did anything to survive and knowing he was useless at body disposal; Arnold played the curse card and completely ransacked the room. He splattered the walls with bloody words, strange texts that he half remembered from old papyrus. He got bandages from the medicine cabinet and left strips torn on the broken windows as if snagged from a fleeing murderer.

The poverty stricken city had no competent law enforcers and the worried men with shields that came to his door retreated quickly with Benjamin's money in their pocket. Only Julia called Arnold a murderer to his face and thousands of miles from home, Arnold didn't care. He had his money and planning permission for his Scottish castle was a go. If Julia hadn't responded to his love letters, then he wouldn't reply to her ridiculous accusations.

At least not until they reached home on different ships and Julia swore to undo all of Arnold's good fortune, she would burn in hell before she let him have her husband's money.

Arnold visited her that night and when she slammed the door in his face and threatened to phone the police–competent law enforcers who would open a proper investigation into her husband's death—then Arnold knew she had signed her own death warrant.

No one could explain the fire that burned Julia's home to the ground. Some spoke of suicide, a result brought on by depression since her husband's death.

Some spoke of curses, the inevitable result of fools breaking sacred seals.

Arnold gave no comment to the police. Of course, he was sad to hear of the sudden deaths of two good friends but he was too busy to attend either's funeral, now that he had a Scottish house to build.

Scotland 1950

Silent, sipping, feeling the world turn, the only men in the old house sat and watched each other, nervously.

"Do you regret killing them?" Richard asked at last, thinking the old man's story was the worst thing he had ever heard.

Arnold shrugged and poured himself more Dutch courage for the coming event. "It was the curse that killed them, son. Not my hands."

Richard nodded; he'd heard that madmen took no responsibility for their action. "And you think some ancient mummy will come tonight and–"

"Do you think I'm stupid, son? I'm a planner, I have foreseen your pettiness," Arnold sneered. He had bested every enemy that fate had set before him, crushing them into the dust, but death was always stronger than flesh. Death always found the hider and ate in the end. "You have your mother's eyes; no doubt that tramp married Benjamin quickly back in twenty-two when she felt her belly swell."

Richard nodded, there was no need for secrets now as he put down his drink and pulled a revolver from his pocket.

A bad sport, Arnold snorted, unimpressed. "I still win, son. I had my fun and spent your parent's money and then took great pleasure in killing them. Their own stubbornness brought about their downfall, if they had just been more charitable, then there wouldn't have been any need for this curse business."

Richard stood and cocked his gun hammer. "This isn't about winning," he said, long promising to mom through prayers that he would not cry in fear or waver in anger. "This is about killing you and nothing else."

Richard fired twice, a brace of rapid explosions that blotted out the thunder. Snorting out the gun smoke, he left the dead man in the chair, keeping only the brandy to give him fuel to help him back to the car.

Damn the rain, he wouldn't spend a night in this old house. Nothing good had come from here. Suddenly, Richard held his head, somehow weak, the gunshots still ringing in his ears, the arsenic the old man had put into the brandy was now beginning to take effect.

Curse of the Ship Burial

E.W. Farnsworth

Doctor Ainsworth and his four crew members drove at dawn to their dig site on the plateau of Giza well outside the extensive area that was reserved for the Great Pyramid. Ainsworth's group was considered to be composed of light-weight archaeologists because they took no interest in producing yet another boring monograph on the stellar orientation of known passages in the pyramids or on the curious absence of visual representations of hieroglyphs inside those supposedly 5,000-year-old monuments.

Instead, they were digging in ground that was presumed to hold, at most, odd shards and remnants of the tool work that, over centuries, had created the giant stones that formed the structure and facing of the pyramids. If Sir Flinders Petrie had scoffed at digging there, how could the acknowledged experts of Egyptian antiquities do otherwise?

Ainsworth was not concerned about what others thought about his work. He had been focused on the site ever since a discovery in the wrappings of a mummy found in the Valley of the Kings. The find had been unquestionably verified by laboratory analysis but because no one could explain its presence in an

Egyptian tomb that had been carbon-dated at 2550 BCE, it had been ignored.

Ainsworth had written speculative papers on the find, but he could not find a reputable publisher for them. Editors' comments included words like rubbish, trashy, shoddy, irresponsible, and the worst phrase of all, 'reprehensible from a supposedly responsible member of the Egyptian scholarly community.' Yet the idea of tobacco leaves having been found in the wrappings of an Egyptian mummy four thousand years before Columbus's discovery of America held an implication that Ainsworth found ineluctable through the received scholarly tradition. It required a new approach.

Only by excavating proof in the form of artifacts would Ainsworth's theories hold any weight. He had considered writing fictional works about his theory under a pseudonym, but if he were ever discovered to be the man behind the fictional name, he would be ridiculed out of his profession and never regarded seriously again.

What brought Ainsworth to look at the site along the southern boundary of the plain surrounding the Great Pyramid was a set of images made by airborne ground-penetrating radar indicating what looked like a giant ship buried under sand and stone tailings. He had worked with imagery analysts of the American Navy to produce from the radar image a scale drawing of the outline of the object buried at the site. Unable to find a sponsor in the United States, Ainsworth went to Europe where he pitched his theory and showed his preliminary evidence to a Dutch princess who liked both him and his idea.

The princess provided seed funding for Ainsworth to prepare a very professional, one-time brief about his proposed project for other royalty friends and eccentric relatives of hers throughout Europe. She used her own considerably persuasive powers at the brief to line up funding for a five-person dig with a ten-year duration. Then she personally lobbied the resident antiquities director in Egypt to fast-track the process for approval of the project. Ironically, approval came because the project was deemed not to be a serious, scholarly expedition but the whim of a European princess.

Finally, the princess presided over the ribbon-cutting that initiated the actual archaeological work. In the press, the event was considered so insignificant that it received only a few lines of mention in the Dutch press. A stock photo of the princess in all her finery was used to accompany the text because the Dutch royal family did not approve of the photo showing her appearing next to 'her explorer' and the Egyptian antiquities director in their expeditionary costumes with dust on their garments and sweat stains from the blast-furnace winds that caused the sweltering desert heat.

The princess returned to her native land and received Ainsworth's annual reports until her untimely, tragic death by an unaccountable illness. She was only thirty years old when she died.

She was not the only one to die in a mysterious, untimely fashion. Within six months of her death, the antiquities director who had posed in the picture taken at the opening of the dig site dropped dead in his office in Cairo. Around the same time, two of Ainsworth's four crew members had been stricken with a disease that was still undiagnosed, but they had recovered from their near-fatal illnesses and were now in the field again with their major professor. Ainsworth himself and his other two workers had some symptoms, but they were never hospitalized. Ainsworth joked with his team that what saved them from certain death of the dread disease that had killed the others was their habit of smoking cigarettes. The professor and his crew averaged three packs a day each, and each year they laid in not cartons but boxes of Marlboro cigarettes that ended up as part of the stash in their tents near the Giza plateau.

It was in the fourth year of their dig that Ainsworth knew that his theory held significant weight because he had verified that the object shown in the aerial radar imagery was indeed an enormous ship, larger than any Egyptian ship known to have existed from historical and archaeological records. In fact, the ship was larger than any known to have been built until the time of the Spanish Armada in the late Sixteenth Century.

Ainsworth once again enlisted the help of the U.S. Navy to do detailed design drawings from the artifact that his team had unearthed. The two naval engineers, who worked with him at the direct order of the Chief of Naval Operations, had experience doing detailed drawings of Noah's ark from biblical records and the archaeological finds high up on Mount Ararat.

They told Ainsworth that they were astounded by the find because the Egyptian vessel would have had the strength and carrying capacity to sustain voyages not just up and down the Nile River and in the Eastern Mediterranean Sea but all over the world. It was their judgment that from the time of Noah to the time of the building of this buried ship, shipbuilding had undergone a radical transformation. They thought that such a transformation would only have been possible in a prolonged age of enlightenment and stress much like the period the world had recently witnessed in the Twentieth Century, which against a backdrop of two world wars, had birthed supertankers, aircraft carriers, and cargo container ships.

Ainsworth used the design drawings to catalyze funding for the reconstruction of the Egyptian vessel, but the new Egyptian antiquities director took umbrage with the archaeologist's project and tried to shut it down on a pretext. Temporarily, the project was shut down and Ainsworth and his people were forbidden to return to the site until 'certain matters' were deliberated at 'appropriate levels'. Ainsworth was not faint of heart, so he decided to continue his work clandestinely through poring through scholarly records all over the world.

He targeted the fabled Vatican Library chart, a copy of much earlier documents, that featured an Antarctic Continental chart showing the medial fissure of that continent that had only in the late Twentieth Century been determined by advanced scientific means.

That meant to Ainsworth that at some point within the last five thousand years Antarctica had been ice-free and that some nautical power had the technology to do the charting necessary to produce the artifact that finally was transposed to become the artifact in the Vatican Library in the days of Henry the Navigator in the late Fifteenth Century. Of course, the Vatican curia buried the manuscript chart because it was entirely too controversial to copy and deliver to the public. Only privileged members of the black Collegium Romanum were permitted to see and analyze the chart. Since the records of the Collegium Romanum were still, in the Twentieth Century, kept closely-held among the curial office, Ainsworth hit a brick wall in his attempts to discover Catholic analysis of the chart.

Ainsworth went to visit the library archives of the world's greatest tobacco companies to discover any record of tobacco growth outside America throughout antiquity. He found no such record, and he was told by the more intelligent and imaginative archivist, who was a scion of the fabled Duke family in America, that only a few channels by which tobacco seeds and products could have been conveyed to Asia or Europe existed until the arrival of Columbus in America in 1492.

One channel was very early and retraced the migration route of the earliest inhabitants of America, who came from Asia via the Bering Strait land bridge ten-thousand years ago. The other channel was Nordic and occurred during the Tenth or Eleventh Century AD.

The possibility of an Egyptian channel for transmission of tobacco products was thought remote, but not impossible. Ainsworth's discovery in Giza intrigued the imaginative archivist enough to incentivize his briefing the wise people of the Duke family about his ideas. It was not luck, but good business sense that brought about the Duke family's funding of Ainsworth's project to build a replica of the ship whose remains he had found in Egypt. Funding was generous enough to support not only the building of the ship but its testing and operational trials that led to experimentation to determine its durability at sea.

The result of Ainsworth's project was proof that a vessel such as the one he built could have explored waters from the Arctic to the Antarctic and from Egypt to China in the third millennium BC. As Thor Heyerdahl in his Kon-Tiki adventure, Ainsworth and his team actually conducted the voyages that proved the Egyptian vessel's potential.

Even in spite of the acclaim Ainsworth's proofs made in the open press, the Egyptian archeological stalwarts remained uniformly opposed to Ainsworth's 'quirky and unprofessional approach'. Where, they asked, were the documentary records proving that the Egyptians had a program of navigational exploration that encompassed an area beyond the Eastern Mediterranean Sea? Ainsworth, to his credit, agreed that capability did not translate into accomplishment, and he sought further evidence to advance his theory.

While he was probing the earliest discovered Egyptian records for evidence of some secret, prior Egyptian history involving global navigation, Ainsworth suffered the tragic loss by a mysterious disease of his chief researcher, Mabel Davies. The young woman died in agony of a disease that apparently had no diagnosis. When Ainsworth asked his worker's doctors to look for commonalities among the symptoms first presented by both the Dutch princess and the director of Egyptian antiquities in Cairo, they admitted that similarities existed, but the medical guilds persons still were clueless as to the nature and cause of the disease that had killed them all. Ainsworth recovered from his grief. Having no replacement for Ms. Davies, he took on her workload himself.

Ainsworth shifted his strategy after Ms. Davies's death. He began looking for things that might tangentially prove his theory such as the incidence of mysterious deaths among ancient peoples. He particularly sought evidence of disease that had no prior counterparts in the medical record.

He discovered in tablets of Mesopotamia the earliest mention of an army's encountering an unknown disease that decimated its ranks and threw the balance in favor of their enemies. Formerly it was thought among medical historians that the disease had been the earliest record of the black plague, but Ainsworth was not at all sure of that. The stone tablet that recorded the ravages of the disease did not have the detail or language that would allow a determination, only the disease's ultimate effect, which was an enemy's victory in battle.

Biological warfare in the third millennium BC might have been possible, but Ainsworth thought another cause might have been just as likely. Forensics was impossible because all the combatants had died and their bodies had returned to dust, but the mummy of the pharaoh who had been wrapped in tobacco leaves remained. Ainsworth arranged with the still-hostile Egyptian director for antiquities to have a sample from the mummy sent for analysis at the USAMRIID in Maryland. His successful argument for the analysis was based on the three deaths that had occurred surrounding his investigations. Ainsworth threatened to give a press conference at which he would allege that ancient Egypt had been so beset with plagues that it was dangerous for anyone to do archaeological research until the possible threat of plague could be explicitly eliminated. He further stated that he would sue the Egyptian government and the antiquities director personally for the losses they and their families had sustained due to the mysterious illness that had caused their deaths.

Ainsworth's sample went to USAMRIID, but he was informed shortly after the analysis began that the sample and all derivatives had been labeled Biological Warfare Level 5 (BL-5) status. That meant that what the scientists had found in the sample they had been given was so lethal that it had to be handled with the highest security levels possible. USAMRIID wanted to seize the mummy and any other samples deriving from it wherever they might be.

A team of four men and three women combed the world for possible derivatives while the U.S. government had consultations directly with the Egyptian government about the disposition of the mummy itself. Finally after significant negotiations and many meetings, the USAMRIID scientists were allowed to take custody of the young pharaoh's mummy and his coffin and all other artifacts that had been discovered in the tomb in the Valley of the Kings where the mummy had been found.

They extended their immediate impoundment to the lab that had done the analysis for the initial discovery of tobacco leaf in the wrappings. In the process of their assessment, USAMRIID scientists found a trail of mysterious deaths, six total at the lab that had found the tobacco and five others at the Egyptian Museum of Antiquities where the mummy and coffin had been stored.

Ainsworth himself was kept in the loop on what was becoming an urgent epidemiological containment exercise. He was the archeologist who knew the most about the history and storage of the artifacts, and he had lost a key researcher to the cause though he and his other colleagues remained alive. Doctor Anne Wayland, the epidemiologist on the USAMRIID team, spent long hours discussing the history of the project with Ainsworth, and in exchange for the information Ainsworth gave the woman, she gave him periodic reports on the ongoing investigation into the cause of the outbreak.

For example, Wayland informed Ainsworth that an extremely rare virus was the imputed cause of all the recorded deaths. It's only counterparts were viruses found in bodies of fresh water in the Arctic that had only recently become accessible for analysis on account of global warming. Ainsworth asked the woman whether the same virus had been found in any core samples from Antarctica, and she seemed shocked that he should ask that question since, indeed, one secret group in USAMRIID was working on analysis with preliminary results suggesting just that.

She said the project was highly classified so she could not go into generalities. She swore Ainsworth to secrecy about it because Chinese and Russian involvement in aspects of the secret research included top-level biological warfare engineers who were thought to have been weaponizing the virus illegally as well as developing a vaccine.

Ainsworth asked Wayland whether any forensics on early American Indian artifacts had been done along the lines that were used on the Egyptian relics. She said she knew of no such efforts, but she thought that if the virus was extant in the Americas, unaccountable deaths should have been much in evidence. She said that any large-scale epidemic or waves of epidemics might have driven the virus out of the Indian blood lines making the survivors immune to any continuing ravages of the disease. She said other factors might have been involved.

When Ainsworth pressed her on this, she said that one of the lab workers, a heavy smoker of cigarettes and cigars, told his cohorts that he probably had the best protection against the virus—his being a heavy smoker. His colleagues had jibed at him for his jocularity in such a serious pursuit, but he told them he was very serious about what he said. He stated that tobacco had a curative value that society had forgotten in the prospect of lung cancer. Doctor Wayland shook her head at the idea.

Ainsworth thought about this theory for a while, and he emailed Wayland that among those he knew had made contact with the artifacts, only the heavy smokers, himself included, had survived. The Dutch princess and the Egyptian director of antiquities had been non-smokers, and his assistant researcher had been trying to stop smoking in the months before she contracted the disease. He said that the USAMRIID team should probably check on the smoker status of all those who had presumably died of the mysterious disease. Wayland meticulously ordered her team to do as Ainsworth requested, and she reported to Ainsworth that all who had died were non-smokers. All colleagues of those who died were smokers who consumed two to three packs of cigarettes each day.

Ainsworth brooded over this evidence, and he decided to visit a cultural anthropologist friend from his graduate student days. The man specialized in early American customs. He was a chain smoker who had for many years been fascinated by the use of tobacco among American Indians before the arrival of Columbus. Ainsworth and Doctor Clyde Forsythe met at a smokers' bar and enjoyed cigars while they talked.

"You're probably going to laugh at what I have to ask, but does your research in pre-Columbian tobacco usage indicate that tobacco was used as a cure for pandemic disease?"

"Francis, that is what my whole line of research has indicated, but I cannot publish what I have found because I have no hard evidence. Besides, as a smoker, my non-smoking colleagues would say I was doing special pleading to use the argument."

"So, Clyde, what if I told you that I know of a virus that could only have been active around five thousand years ago in the Americas and that evidence of the virus extends from the North Pole to the South Pole? Wait a minute—don't laugh, there's more. What if I told you that the only people who have survived contact with the virus in our time are heavy smokers just like us?"

"You're baiting me, right? What have you been smoking? No kidding though, if what you say is true, it would surely make my day. Why, I could publish my work tomorrow, and no one could laugh at my thesis."

"Now that I've let you in on the secret—and for now, this is just between us—I have to ask whether you know of anything that might indicate from American pre-Columbian history that tobacco might have been used, say, to protect a dead body from the pandemic in the afterlife. I would expect remains in tombs, for example, and in stone representations or manuscripts."

"I see that you are serious about this. Instead of firing from the hip, I'll stop what I am researching right now and dig through the artifacts and records to see what fits your vision."

"Look, everyone knows about Indians smoking peace pipes and using tobacco in ceremonies. I'm going to give you, in confidence, another piece of this puzzle. My project in Egypt has focused on the remains of tobacco in the wrappings of the mummy of a pharaoh that was interred in the Valley of the Kings around twenty-five hundred BC. I found in debris around the plateau of Giza the remains of a ship."

"Yes, I've been following the voyages you and your team have taken to prove how extensively the Egyptians possibly traded and colonized around the world. I've frankly wondered whether those Egyptians managed to make it to America. Now you link tobacco in the mix with scientific evidence. I have to go back to square one to examine whether any but the most obvious connections can be drawn between American Indians and Egyptians."

"So what do you mean by 'obvious connections'?"

"Pyramids, for one. Writing in hieroglyphics for another. Some burial customs. Architecture. Many things in Indian culture could not have come from Asia. Most scholarship puts western contact too late to have had influence before the Vikings."

"If the Egyptians sailed all over the world in ships that could have reached America not just once but many times over the period, let's say, of a few centuries, could those contacts have left the influences that you cannot otherwise explain."

"Carl Jung 'explained' the connections as belonging to the archetypes in all humans, but I've never bought into that. It's absurd. Why if that were true, why didn't American Indians invent the wheel? It's just like tobacco. You have to transport the plant or the seeds; otherwise, you cannot have tobacco in two widely divergent places any more than you can have a rhinoceros herd without a mating pair to start with."

"I have two points of connection; the tobacco and the virus, and I believe those two are themselves connected, the one being the cure for the other. I am struggling to put everything together, but I have some evidence that somehow Egyptians carried both the virus and the tobacco back to their own country after they obtained them here in America. They did not realize at first how the two connected, but whole armies died of the virus—I think I have a contemporary record of that. In Egypt, some magician put two and two together and realized that tobacco was the cure, but all the Egyptian traders brought home were the leaves of the plant, not the seeds. So the precious leaves could be used to protect the pharaoh from the virus in the afterlife, but it could not protect the people from dying in a great pandemic. From the Egyptian point of view, the cause of the dread disease was the transoceanic contact with distant foreigners."

"So—let me guess—the priests inveigh against the whole enterprise of worldwide commerce because all it was bringing home was death and destruction in invisible agents that no one understood. The priests convinced the panicking hierarchies that unless overseas transport stopped forthwith, civilization would become extinct."

"Precisely, so they ordered the great ships to be buried and all records and other evidence of their use to be destroyed. The only evidence they could not destroy were the ships themselves and the tobacco that was used in the pharaoh's mummy wrappings."

"I can see why the mummy survived. The Valley of the Kings was thought to be super-secret, booby-trapped, and such with all the grave preparers killed. Why not burn the ships instead of interring them?"

"Evidently, the priests did not see the ships as being the problem, only their use in foreign trade. There might have been a thousand reasons for discontinuing the building of those ships. Perhaps their designers and builders died of the pandemic. Perhaps there was a problem with financing such ships when the Egyptians began conquering other land powers and used their captives as slaves to build the pyramids. Perhaps the genius sailors that piloted those ships had died without successors. Who knows why the ships could no longer be used. The critical thing from the priests' point of view was that they should not be used for long-haul transit any longer. What did the Egyptians do with things whose use had died? They interred them."

"So you've found no Book of the Dead for ships? As I recall, E. A. Wallace Budge's translation mentions a number of boats that were used in funeral rites."

"Yes, Nilotic crafts that were extremely small vessels by comparison with those that were used for transoceanic travel. Think of the difference between a hearse in a funeral cortege and a supertanker on the high seas. I've thought through every reference to water travel in the Book of the Dead and in all the pictures in Egyptian tombs, but only one fits the pattern I'm looking for."

"Then your boat must be the one rowed by the Grateful Dead."

"You've got a point. Only the grateful dead row a celestial vessel through the heavens for eternity. The rock group of the same name took their name from that passage in Budge, and it has haunted me throughout this project. How could the Egyptians have possibly come to that conception except by having at some time sailed and rowed around the known world? For the minute, forget the circumnavigation aspect and think of long-haul voyages. Perhaps with colonization. And, of course, transport of exotica back from foreign climes for the pharaoh's personal use."

"Yet, besides the tobacco, you have no artifact to bring to the fight?"

"None with the compelling argument behind it that tobacco has."

"I'll do some research in this line because it can help both of us, and if I find anything you might find useful, I'll let you know."

Something in the conversation he had with Clyde struck Ainsworth as being significant, but he could not put his finger on what it was right away. Some weeks had passed before he discovered what made him uncomfortable; it was Clyde's statement about the Grateful Dead. If, he thought, the ancient Egyptians had been so struck with long-haul voyaging that they had made a fundamental reference to it in the Book of the Dead, their most ancient and sacred record for the afterlife, then perhaps the referent for the boat that the Grateful Dead had rowed might be the one that he had uncovered near Giza. There were boats that suggested the heavenly voyage in tomb paintings, but nothing explicitly linking the heavenly voyage to an earthly one. Could it be that the reason that the boat had been interred was that it could then continue in its service after its own lifespan just as for humans mummification served the purpose? All this was pure speculation, but Ainsworth wanted to stretch the limits of his imagination in case such brainstorming led to an insight that he could use in his archeological work.

When the Egyptian director of antiquities decided that earning money was preferable to holding a grudge, Doctor Ainsworth returned with his crew to the Giza site where the ship he had found now lay under an enormous canopy. To either side of the excavation area lay enormous earthworks of sand and rocks that had been removed to uncover the ship. To support the hull of the ancient ship, wooden struts and supports had been introduced. Within the artificial underground area around the ship was a perimeter path of three meters in width. Ainsworth walked the path with his crew examining the walls carefully for signs of a hidden chamber or entry to a chamber.

Nothing looked promising along the walls, but on the floor that had been uncovered and swept clear in the excavation process, three areas seemed to be covered with large apparently flat stones that had been cut to measure. On impulse, Ainsworth directed his crew to clear the edges around one of those stones and fit a pry bar in the space that they created in doing so.

Using the pry bar with much effort, they lifted the stone and saw that an empty volume lay under it.

Having removed the stone entirely, they saw an incline leading downwards. Never shy about pursuing a new avenue, Ainsworth grabbed a torch, jumped into the opening and proceeded down the incline with his crew following close behind him with their torches.

Typically, they all kept smoking their cigarettes as they went down the thirty feet to a level floor that opened into a gigantic underground room that was cut out of the native rock under the plateau. What they found there astounded them because nothing quite like it existed in any of the scholarly literature about ancient Egypt.

On all four vertical walls were painted pictures of Egyptians landing in a ship like the one they had uncovered on apparently foreign shores. They recognized the tobacco plant growing among other American foliage to the left, which was the western wall. They recognized figures that looked Chinese coming to greet the voyagers on the east wall. On the north wall were figures whose bodies were painted blue and red. Ainsworth guessed those would have been ancestors of the Picts in what today was Scotland. He recognized nothing in the mural on the south wall except for what looked like a stylized penguin. Perhaps that was supposed to be Antarctica. Looking up at the ceiling of the room, the crew made out constellations oriented in such a way that the cardinal directions indicated by the walls could be verified against celestial signs.

"A little world made cunningly," Ainsworth said to his crew. Then he told them to fetch the camera gear.

They had only three hours to do their photographs and then close up the area where they had entered this room because it was clearly beyond the boundaries that had been established for their dig. Under Egyptian law, they could be prosecuted for trespassing and grave robbing if they should be discovered here.

While his people made the photographs, Ainsworth used a sketch pad to make notes about the dimensions of the room and the approximate sizes of the major images there. Here was all the proof he would need to make his transformative case to the scholarly world and change the course of Egyptology irrevocably.

The crew knew the enormity of the find as well as their leader. They were recording, they were convinced, the counterpart of Tutankhamen's tomb. The years of their lives that had been devoted to working with the professor had finally paid off, and they would be featured in the history books. So when they retreated from the room back up the incline to the area where the ship lay on its supports, they were both exhausted and exhilarated.

They chain lit their cigarettes and began to talk excitedly now where in the depths of their new find they had worked in tense silence. They carefully placed the flat stone back over the hole that led to the incline and the room. At Ainsworth's direction, they then swept sand into the cracks around the edges of the stone so that the entry would be difficult for anyone else to discover. Ainsworth said that they should meet at his tent for a brief discussion before they did anything else.

At their meeting in his tent, the first thing Ainsworth told his crew was that they had made history. He congratulated them and thanked them for their hard work and their faith in their common vision. He then stated that what they had found could not be made public until they had gained permission to extend their dig to include the volume of the room.

For many reasons, he explained, early disclosure would jeopardize not only their future access and permission to publish but also their ability to enter and leave the nation of Egypt as they saw fit. Early discovery would essentially make them outlaws; they would be pilloried as desecrators of Egypt's sacred heritage. It did not matter, he said, how important their find was or how crucial it was for them to be the ones to announce and interpret it. They would have to be patient and stage the revelation of the room they had found carefully. He swore each person individually to silence, and he collected all their cameras so that he could have the films that they contained developed by a special expert he had often used. She had the ability to keep a secret indefinitely.

He said he would be departing with the evidence on the first flight out of Cairo the next afternoon. He ordered the others to break their tents and depart in a leisurely fashion not later than four days after he had left. He asked them all to rendezvous at his university campus office in one week.

Ainsworth felt light headed from his discovery because it confirmed everything that he surmised and more. He was exceptionally watchful just in case someone became suspicious and sent a watchdog after him to find out why he had departed earlier than the Egyptian authorities expected.

In fact, his early departure was noticed by the USAMRIID team, who met him at the airport and accompanied him back to the U.S. When they were back in America, the team leader told Ainsworth that he should accompany him to visit the USAMRIID facility in Maryland to discuss the latest developments in the viral research that was being conducted.

Ainsworth did not feel constrained by USAMRIID's request. In fact, he was interested in getting an update, and he felt he needed a change of pace to calm down and gain perspective on his latest find.

When he arrived at USAMRIID, he was greeted cordially by the director and technical director, both of whom thanked him for coming on short notice. They then led him into an underground conference center where they offered him coffee and donuts and told him that they had three hours of briefings for him if he had the time to experience them. Ainsworth told them he was agreeable, and the show began.

The evidence at first appalled Ainsworth and then alarmed him. The number of unaccountable deaths surrounding his dig and the artifacts associated with it had gone asymptotic. Over three hundred people had died and another thousand were identified as affected. Of those who were known to have contracted the illness, the death rate was ninety percent. The incubation period for the illness was between two and four years, so the virus had the longest incubation and highest lethality of any previously known predator on the human species.

USAMRIID's epidemiologist reported the predictive analytic data indicating that within the next five years over five million persons would have contracted the new plague, and four and a half million of those would perish. She explained that the USAMRIID scientists were scrambling to produce a vaccine, but the virus seemed to mutate as fast as their research so that when they developed a potential vaccine, the virus had segued to a new strain that was invulnerable when confronted with the vaccine that had been produced.

USAMRIID had never recorded a faster rate of structural change in another virus. Even flu could not compare. The problem, she said, was that no one would believe that the virus was natural. All the major nations would think that the virus had escaped from a biological warfare development program gone amok. That put the U.S. in a difficult position. What they needed was a strategy to let the world know that the source of the virus was not a biowar lab but an archaeological expedition with momentous implications not only for the past but for the future.

Ainsworth listened carefully to what the epidemiologist said, and he saw the director and technical director nod their heads in agreement with her judgment. The director thanked the epidemiologist for her presentation and asked her to leave the room while he talked with Ainsworth with his technical director.

When she had departed, the director turned to Ainsworth and told him that he had become a party to information that, if divulged outside the room they were in, would render grave damage to the United States. He, therefore, insisted that Ainsworth sign national security papers indoctrinating him into a named caveat and granting him a top secret clearance.

The papers he signed pledged him not to divulge anything about the virus's origin or its spread to anyone unless the information was approved in advance by USAMRIID in writing. Ainsworth realized that he did not have a choice but to comply, so he did so. With the stroke of a pen his academic freedom disappeared. His chance to publish what he had found went to zero. When he had left Egypt, he had felt he was on the brink of announcing the discovery of the millennium. Now he felt he had been forced to betray his mission and his crew because of national security.

When he signed the papers, Doctor Ainsworth was informed that he was now working for USAMRIID full time and that his university would be informed to grant him a sabbatical of indefinite scope and duration while he performed duties necessary for the security of the United States. He was told that his Dean had already agreed to the terms. He was also told that his colleagues and crew would be informed by the government that he was on special assignment. In this way, the archeologist became part of the USAMRIID's epidemiological team to fight against the spread of the dread disease that unintentionally he had been instrumental in releasing upon the world.

Now it was Ainsworth's turn to brief the USAMRIID team on his findings including his latest discoveries. He was told that he should admit nothing because of the critical importance of what he had done. He was also told that his latest discovery was the most important part of his briefing since it may have opened an entirely new dimension of the emerging threat. So Ainsworth was permitted to collect his thoughts for seventy-two hours and to compile a brief that gave first the history of his dig, then the sequence of his discoveries and finally the thoughts he had about how what he found came together into a coherent vision of how the virus had affected its environment historically up to the present moment.

Ainsworth realized that, classified as the brief would be, it was the closest he would ever come to publishing his findings. It no longer seemed to matter that publication would be to a very small audience of listeners. What mattered most was how USAMRIID could mobilize the world's medical community to combat the disease that was killing people quietly in ways no other epidemic had ever done.

Ainsworth's brief, which is still highly classified, was a tour de force. In the opening three slides, he focused his audience on his grand theory about the presence of the large ship burial at Giza. In the subsequent five slides, he showed how his team had accomplished their excavation and what they found at each stage of their work. The final slide in this part of his three-part sequence included a montage of the photographs his team had taken within the subterranean room under the Giza plateau. The photographs had been developed by a special USAMRIID team devoted to the purpose of assisting the professor in compiling his brief. Ainsworth concluded his brief with statistics on the use of tobacco as an antidote to the virus showing that heavy smokers survived while non-smokers perished. His final slide showed his conclusion; the plague induced by the virus ended overnight a centuries-old global nautical exploration enterprise by the ancient Egyptians. Vestiges of this ancient maritime trade could be found in certain documents, but ultimate proofs could only be found in the subterranean room that he and his team had discovered but not yet disclosed or published because of complications of the means of discovery.

The director of USAMRIID requested a copy of the brief, and when he received it, he flew to Washington, DC, where he briefed the slides to the Director of National Security and the National Security Council. His presentation was a resounding success, and he was invited to deliver the same brief to the Director of National Intelligence, who took the USAMRIID director directly to the President of the United States.

Meanwhile at USAMRIID HQ, Ainsworth refined and amplified his brief and worked with the epidemiological team on a strategy for combating the virus using tobacco in a wide variety of ways. Because of his conviction that tobacco could cure the root cause of the disease, he became a guinea pig for the agency. Increasingly concentrated samples of the virus were injected into his veins and his blood was withdrawn every six hours to determine how his antibodies attacked the virus. At the same time, he was encouraged to chain smoke throughout his waking hours. He was also subjected to compresses and poultices of ground tobacco, which were applied to various parts of his body to test their maximum effectiveness by location. Ainsworth lived through this experimentation, and he asked whether USAMRIID had used a control in parallel with him. He was informed that the female epidemiologist had heroically volunteered to be the control, but she had contracted the virus after the second week and was now in critical condition in the USAMRIID medical facility. She was not expected to survive.

Ainsworth was outraged, and he demanded that the woman be given tobacco instantly to thwart the virus. He was told that she refused to use any tobacco products because they were harmful to a person's health. So Ainsworth realized that a Catch-22 situation had arisen and that there was no way to break the deadlock as long as the woman's will was still in the equation. The woman died of the virus and received a posthumous commendation for her self-sacrifice.

Ainsworth, however, was defiant and denounced USAMRIID's methods and purpose. The director of USAMRIID told Ainsworth to prepare a scholarly article about his discoveries so that the government could explain through it to the people just how the virus had entered the present world from the ancient one.

Ainsworth did as he was ordered to do, and then he gave his paper to USAMRIID rewrite experts, who tailored his paper to their needs. They explained that there would be no need to have his paper refereed in the usual manner for scholarly papers because USAMRIID had its own ways to deliver information to the public. Ainsworth's paper was published in a top epidemiological journal. In the revised version that was published, Ainsworth was made to appear like a rabid archeologist who would do anything for his own fame. His hubris had led him to a seemingly impossible thesis that turned out to be true but backfired on him and others when a virus hidden in an artifact escaped and began multiplying among the innocent populace.

Ainsworth was distraught with the substance of the article, but the public outcry against him and his team was savage and indignant. Overnight he became a villain both in the U.S. and abroad. USAMRIID put out the word that it had contained Doctor Ainsworth to get to the bottom of how exactly he had orchestrated the escape of the virus. The agency made it sound as if he had been made a prisoner who would be punished by the government behind a cloak of secrecy.

Meanwhile, Egypt flew into a diplomatic rage over the allegation that its ancient forebears had ever ventured on water beyond the Blue and White Nile, the Nile Delta and the eastern Mediterranean Sea. The Egyptian authorities demanded a brief from USAMRIID on their secret findings so that an appropriate public rebuttal could be formulated. They also rescinded the dig permit that had been granted to Ainsworth and his team and closed off his dig site from public access. Ainsworth's university expelled him from the faculty and initiated legal action against him for using his affiliation with the university in his infamous article. His crew was summarily dismissed from the university as accomplices.

When Ainsworth protested that he had been treated unfairly by his host agency, he was informed by the director that any formal protest by an employee of USAMRIID must be registered with him first and he would block it's going forward on the grounds of national security. When he objected to what had been published in his name, he was told that the difference between what had been published and what he had briefed was due to reductions in the name of national security and that, as such, offered no grounds for a formal objection. Essentially Ainsworth became a scapegoat and a tool of USAMRIID.

When he tried to make people understand the importance of tobacco in the solution, he was told that it was impossible to use tobacco in any form because of U.S. health policy. How could the public be told that smoking would help them survive the plague when they had been brainwashed to think that any use of tobacco was tantamount to taking a poisoned pill? So Ainsworth realized that the tobacco connection was a non-starter.

Fortunately, he was allowed to continue to smoke. In fact, the endless supply of tobacco products was the one blessing in the whole mess that USAMRIID created around him.

Every two weeks Ainsworth was briefed on the progress of the plague, and after that briefing he was tasked to brief his minders about what he had discovered in the interval since his last brief. Ainsworth realized that what he said would not be regarded seriously, so he extrapolated on his findings in wildly imaginative ways. He used the imagery he had seen in the room that, he presumed, no longer existed. He explored the connections that his friend Clyde had suggested to draw the ancient world of Egypt together with pre-Columbian America. He drew parallels between the virulent reactions of the ancient Egyptians to international navigation and the virulent reactions of USAMRIID to the global extent of the plague. No one listened to him. Instead, in their briefings they reported that all of Ainsworth's crew had died under mysterious circumstances that may or may not have been related to the plague.

Ainsworth's friend Clyde had also succumbed even though he was an inveterate smoker and, in the good doctor's opinion, should never have perished. In the briefings, the numbers of victims of the plague were reported to have reached over one hundred million because the plague had reached China and Japan.

Each nation accused the other of deploying a biological weapon to destroy its people. The Vatican meanwhile denounced the kind of archaeological forensics that would bring a plague upon humankind. So once again the Collegium Romanum went to work to bury all evidence that Ainsworth had adduced.

An international group comprised of altruists and billionaires demanded that new archaeological investigations around the Giza plateau should be vetted through the United Nations prior to their authorization. This guaranteed that no new digs would be authorized until the measures were relaxed. When archaeologists asked about opportunities for them to examine Doctor Ainsworth's site, they were told that the site had been condemned and dismantled and that the artifacts, including the mummy, the coffin, the ship and the murals were destroyed because of the threat of the plague.

An outcry went up from the entire archaeological community at the sacrilege of willful destruction of historical artifacts, but the public in a frenzy whipped up by the international media insisted that the people involved in the studies that had released the virus be prosecuted to the fullest extent of the law. Jurists speculated on instituting the death penalty for just such offenses.

The health industry, noting that tobacco had been invoked as a possible cure for the virus, assailed the very idea that tobacco could be an effective weapon in the war on the plague. The AMA threatened to sue Ainsworth for practicing medicine without a license and to sue USAMRIID for publicizing Ainsworth's nefarious views on tobacco, which everyone knew caused cancer and was no cure for anything.

The plague raged on while the international health community did everything but find an effective vaccine for the virus. Nature found a cure when the institutions of humankind failed to do so. Analysis showed that the virus mutated so fast that before a year had passed, it no longer had any of the characteristics with which it started. Its virulence dropped to twenty-five percent lethality, then ten percent, then one percent.

Finally, the virus was not killing victims but only incapacitating them for, at maximum, a week, the symptoms reduced to a mild headache and nausea. The plague had burned itself out, and only two hundred million people had perished.

USAMRIID took the credit for conquering the dread disease, and Ainsworth was dismissed from service with USAMRIID because he was no longer needed now that the pandemic was over. Panic in the press was transformed into retrospection. Now the even-handed analysts began sifting through all the evidence looking for lessons that could be learned so that humanity would not have to go through the kind of torture that the virus had represented ever again.

An investigative reporter found Ainsworth working at a Wal-Mart store in Cincinnati and asked him whether he would do what he did again knowing what he now knew. Ainsworth screwed up his mouth and said he might, but he would not want to give up smoking in any case. The article that the reporter wrote was spiked by his editor on account of the remark quoted about smoking. It was the newspaper's policy not to promote statements that encouraged smoking even obliquely. The reporter was a fighter, so he sold his article as a freelancer to a North Carolina newspaper that was tobacco friendly.

The same investigative reporter traveled to Egypt to see what had happened to Ainsworth's dig site. He discovered that there had never been such a site. The director of antiquities drove him to the area where the site was supposed to be, and it was an enormous new parking lot for fleets of tourist buses. The reporter could see that flocks of people were arriving to visit the Great Pyramid now that the threat of plague had been lifted. The reporter was savvy, and he asked the director of antiquities what had happened to the ship burial that had been discovered near the Giza plateau. At this idea, the director shook his head.

Egypt, he explained with a sigh, had never been known to bury ships. In the Valley of the Kings, they had buried many mummies, yes, and many of those could be seen in the local museums. Of course, he said, there were boats that went up and down the Nile just as they did today. He said that ancient Egyptians wrote about the sun as if it were a great ship that the dead rowed through the sky. That was recorded in the Book of the Dead. As for the rumors of ship burials, the rumors themselves were a curse.

The reporter rejoined that the plague was real and many millions of people died.

The director looked sad and said he regretted very much that people died, but what can humans do against a new virus? "And now," the director continued, "the threat has gone away. Do you want to see the Great Pyramid before you leave? I think maybe you have seen enough of the great parking lot."

With that observation, the investigative reporter could not agree more.

Pyramidion

Stephen McQuiggan

Peterson limps through the morass of his nightmares like a broken martinet. Unraveling the kaleidoscopic hieroglyphs that make up his life, twisting and turning as they lash out with a scorpion sting and waking as always with the taste of sand in his mouth. A lull, like a warm zephyr, before he is dragged back down once more.

Before the bleaching sun there were the damp streets of Oxford; before the Mastabas and death palaces there were cricket and cream teas; before Mackay there was Angeline and dancing in the Pavilion.

Dancing.

His fevered mind takes that as an instruction, an imperative–leads him in a slow waltz back to the humid hell of the Delta. Spinning him slowly down the brown fecundity of the Nile away from the pale Angeline and toward the withered face of Professor Mackay, until he is whirring in a manic polka into the dead heart of the camp at Saqqara.

The Professor is expounding his theory of the nature of the secrets of the high priests of Unas and Peterson's mind is still dancing, dancing, dancing…

Dancing like he had the first night they struck camp, full of the local wine Mackay said would rip the hump from a camel; dancing as he cried, his tears 90 proof.

The telegram arrived just as the tents were pitched and they were plotting the dig for the morning; Angeline was dead, her consumptive heart finally placated. Peterson drowned his sorrows, unable to find any other viable connection from this vast barren inferno to the wet and windy land in which she lay. He danced to recall the times he had held her in his arms—so slight she was, like grasping a feather—danced as if he could find a rhythm that could traverse the miles and kick-start her heart.

Mackay had offered him the opportunity to abandon the expedition but reminded him that all that awaited him at home was ennui and despair. At least here the sun could bleach the wrinkles from his brain, smooth it out until no crevasse remained to house her memory.

"Excellent!" declared Mackay when he told him of his decision to stay; "Get it out of your system. Tomorrow we begin. Your vocation is the death of those long gone, and your fiancé belongs to their number now."

The days shuffled by slowly, dancing to their own tune.

"I think the Professor may have the cure for your grief," Gram confided in him later that week, as they brushed the silt of centuries from the faience dishes they had found in the vast birthing house, or Mammisi, of the ancients.

"He has been spending a lot of time studying the reliefs in the Chapel of Min, traveling to Abusir ostensibly to compare fertility charms," his old tutor smiled, "but I can read him like a scroll. When he's excited, he cannot hide it beneath his usual dour mask. And only one thing excited him enough to make the expedition in the first place."

"The resurrection ritual?" Peterson remembered well how the Professor's lectures harped on and on about the occult ceremonies he had discovered in the papyrus fragments purporting to be from the reign of the 5th dynasty King Unas. Pedantic and rambling, the only students left to listen to his fevered outpourings were Peterson himself, and his strange taciturn teacher, Gram.

"Mackay lost someone too," Gram confided, "and I think he hopes to find him here." He indicated the monotone lunar landscape with a desultory shift of his bland eyes. "You're a vital cog my young friend, more vital than you know."

In the days that followed Mackay rarely left Peterson's side and, though the talk was of the cataloging and prosaic organization, more than once he caught the Professor's dry eyes scrutinize him as if he were a piece of anachronistic pottery or an anomalous glyph.

"In the time of Unas the great priests had their own birthing houses, their own vast Mammisi, and what they birthed there had lived many times before in many different guises," said Mackay in measured tones, as if unwilling to lend any weight to his words. "Or so they say," he smiled. "If you could bring back the dead what do you think they would say? Do you think they would thank you?"

"I think I would not care, so long as I had them back."

"And what price would you pay?"

"What price would such a thing cost?" Peterson was growing angry with this childish discourse–the heat had obviously boiled the Professor's already addled wits. He stepped out of the tent and into the moonlight thinking, *What price? Why, I would die myself.*

At sunset, the Mammisi looked like a blank mound of soil, a grave for a giant recently excavated and not yet filled in–or a large boulder holding captive beneath something so primitive, so evil, it could never be named. The steles of Abusir contained hints of what once stalked this region–even the ostracons he had studied—maddeningly vague as they were—held warnings of a seductive unknown terror, some unmentionable obscenity.

Gram stood in the shadow of the mound smoking one of his immaculately rolled cigarettes. "I think our eminent Professor has succumbed to a madness fermented in his grief," said Peterson to him by way of greeting. "I think I shall return to England on the next packet; there's nothing for me here now."

"Yet you're the very reason we are here," said Gram, blowing a twin diabolic stream of smoke from his nostrils. "Do you really believe he brought you on this dig to sup on your meagre income or partake of your massive intellect? You've a keen mind to be sure, but there are plenty of students that tick that box; ones with money in their pocketbooks too. You remind him of the son he lost–that's why you're here. And now your grief ensures you can be trusted to do what must be done."

"And what must be done?"

Gram laughed through a fug of tobacco, "You think we are here to catalogue fertility charms? The British Museum is already crumbling under the weight of broken crockery as it is. Mackay has set his sights on something grander, something that will resound through the ages."

"Resurrection? His madness is more infectious than I thought if you, too, buy into it."

"MacKay is a genius; did you sit through his lectures and think him weak of mind? His brilliance drew you here, of that there is no doubt. Do not make the mistake of doubting him now. This will be the apex, the pyramidion, of his career. Not that his legacy concerns him now–he just wants his boy back."

"I fail to see my role in all of this," sighed Peterson, turning to go as he felt the cold desert beginning to bite.

"When he returns from the Chapel of Min he will have all he needs to attempt the ritual. Your grief will be his link and anchor–a shared lifeline if you will. Then you must do what he cannot, and what I am not equipped to."

"And what is a mediocre student equipped to do that his venerable tutor cannot?"

"To kill him," said Gram, stubbing out his cigarette on the darkening sand.

"Of course!" scoffed Peterson, unable to hide his contempt.

"But you will," Gram assured him quietly, his eyes reflecting the newly risen moon. "It will be a brief death, if a violent one, but you will do it all the same."

"What makes you so sure?"

"Because you yearn to see your little English rose once more."

Peterson went to his tent in silence, unable to bear the ghost of Angeline on his old tutor's lips.

He was summoned to the Mammisi early the next morning. He followed one of the porter's spluttering torches down a steep stairwell hewn into the mercifully cold earth, rehearsing all the while how best to break the news of his imminent departure. Yet when he finally reached the claustrophobic cavern at the stairwell's end and saw Mackay, his hands stained with ochre where he had scratched strange symbols on the crumbling walls, his face thin and haggard in the light of a ring of unforgiving flame, his determination to leave was replaced by instant concern.

Mackay dismissed the porter with a jerk of his gaunt chin as he beckoned Peterson toward a makeshift altar where a few papyrus scrolls flickered in the subterranean breeze.

"Professor—" began Peterson, but Mackay gripped him by the shoulders, his breath as arid as a dust devil, and stopped him in his tracks.

"The time is upon us," Mackay hissed, "watch and listen so that your heart will not falter and our grief will be assuaged. Behold, it is beginning!"

The far wall began to shimmer as the dust swirled into patterns—hexagrams, glyphs, strange angular beasts—before coalescing into the living portrait of a cat that sparkled and trembled, then transformed into the face of an achingly beautiful woman.

"The Goddess Herself," said MacKay in an awed whisper, and at the sound of his voice the divine image turned her haunting kohl-lined eyes upon him until he fell to his knees and bowed his head.

Peterson held his breath, sure the vision was about to speak and that her words would tear him asunder, but the face glimmered once more and changed in an oxygen starved heartbeat until the pale visage of his beloved Angeline peered down upon him wearing her familiar delicate smile.

"Free me," she implored, and Peterson was certain she spoke only in his head; Mackay was still sobbing on his knees, oblivious to the terror in its tone. "Kill the conduit and we will dance again, my love."

Her voice frittered away with her image, leaving only dust motes in place of splendor. Peterson fled the Mammisi, screaming incoherent instructions for the porters to retrieve the Professor. He took refuge in his tent, calming his nerves with whiskey and denial, until sundown when Gram came to escort him to Mackay.

"He is ready, all has been prepared." Gram flashed his nicotine stained teeth in an approximation of a smile; "Remember, the Goddess will test your resolve— her gifts are not given lightly. She will play on your doubts to see if you are worthy. I suggest you leave them here at the bottom of your bottle. Stay strong and you will embrace the one you love once more this night."

The canvas flap fluttered amiably in the searing breeze; a breeze that felt more like e-daemonic breath to Peterson as he surveyed the baked wasteland outside the Professor's tent. The heat had sucked all the life out of the land; only the insistent hum of unseen insects filled the void, a hum like the thrum of blood to a black and diseased heart.

"You know that man in there," Gram was saying, his voice formed, too, of the constant rubbing of insect legs. "He is the best of us all. You are honored and blessed to do this for him."

Peterson nodded numb assent; even his beard hurt, the bristles like needles in the dry tundra of his neck. Yes, MacKay was the best of them, but what good was such a title when he lay strapped to a stone slab behind that rippling flap?

Gram passed him a dull blade, "One quick stab in each eye, then sever the tongue." If Peterson could have summoned up the moisture, he would have wept.

The heat inside the tent stole what little breath remained to him. He stood a moment to gather himself, to regain focus and recall the face of Angeline on the Mammisi's dun wall. He could feel the hilt of the knife blister the skin from his palm as he hesitated. The drone of the insects was muted by the oven blare of heat; only MacKay's rasp was sharp enough to penetrate it.

Peterson kept his eyes on the Professor, ignoring the hieroglyphs of hate and madness daubed on the canvas, and walked toward the slab where Mackay was tightly bound. *It'll be a blessing,* he told himself, *to send him to his son.* In the dim light, Mackay looked emaciated, his skin so waxen it shone; already sand filled the ridges in his deeply lined face.

He looked dead already; only his unblinking eyes showed any signs of animation as they followed Peterson with avid interest, their orbit causing a rustling in their sockets. As Peterson approached Mackay's blanched tongue snaked out like a newborn rat from a puckered womb and tried vainly to moisten his parched and splitting lips.

"You came," said Mackay, and his voice was strong and resonant, vibrating in the air like a distant hint of thunder; Peterson winced at the sewage stench that followed in its wake. "The little Dancing Boy comes to do what he was bid!"

"Yes," said Peterson, aware the insult was a trick to goad him. "I came because I'm your friend."

Mackay's body contorted, shaking with a terminal rattle. For a second he thought he was witnessing the Professor's death throes until he realized it was laughter that convulsed Mackay rather than the grave.

"Friend?" MacKay cackled, spit thick as gruel forming on his bloodless lips. "Friend?" the word sounded like a curse. "Well, get on with it… if you have the stomach for it."

Peterson hefted the blade and drew a scorched breath, feeling the flame of it lick at his protesting lungs.

"Oh, one other thing… Friend… when you take out my eyes you have to eat them, did they tell you that? I hope you choke. And when you do I'll be watching–watching from the inside!" The parody of laughter again, a kindling inferno.

Peterson's face remained emotionless; this was the test then, the one Gram had warned him of. "Of course I was told," he replied evenly.

"And still you came?" The sarcasm in Mackay's voice was layered with a faint feminine echo. "Dancing Boy, who gagged on the local fare, who turned up his puritanical nose at sheep testes, now has a hankering for eyeballs! Oh, Dancing Boy, does this desiccated flesh look like it was born yesterday?"

"Don't call me that."

The Professor chuckled, his body spasming, sending little puffs of sand up into the cloying air.

"I do it for you," Peterson said, "for us both, that we may find peace once more… one way or another." He raised the blade between them, "I do this for you… Even this."

"Before you damn your soul," said Mackay, all strength gone now from his voice, "would you do one last thing for me?"

"Anything."

The Professor's tongue flickered nervously over the moonscape of his lips, "Would you dance one last time? It would mean so much to me."

Peterson fought back a lump in his throat that barred all response. He began to sway slowly, gradually building up speed until he was gyrating, flailing his arms out in sharp counterpoint; and still he danced on, feeling he could never stop, not even if–

Mackay's mocking laughter stopped him abruptly. He raised the knife in a hate fueled rage and, knowing that Mackay was trying to make it easier for him, plunged the blade into the dry ancient orbs of the Professor.

Mackay's eyes tasted like music as they jigged down his throat–and then he was dancing with Angeline again, in a windblown orchard on a rainy August morn; the apples just ripening and the grass soaking the hem of her dress. He hummed as they sashayed from tree to tree, hummed louder than the wasps that sought to keep him from their worm-eaten treasure; but Angeline was the only jewel he craved.

He danced on, for once in his life indifferent to death's sting. He had her in the here and now and that was more than enough.

"I dreamt you were dead," he whispered, "a dream so real… "

"You're so silly," she smiled, and what did it matter if her teeth were rotted and stank of the grave when their hearts beat in unison to the ebb and flow of an unseen orchestra.

"Can the dead kiss like this?" and she pressed her lips, so warm, so alive, to his and his senses overloaded; the sharp twang of decaying fruit, the wet musty aroma of the grass, and the very light of the diluted sun seeming to infuse his blood, making him so giddy he thought he must surely faint.

"Do you love me?" she asked, her words an anchor to the present as the world drifted off into memory; "Tell me you love me."

♌♌♌

Gram watched Peterson stumble from the tent clutching the Professor's ragged corpse. The desert wind had picked up, blowing away the last strands of hair from the old academic's peeling skull and powdering the last strips of flesh from his clattering bones as Peterson whirled the cadaver around and round humming a jaunty show tune.

His eyes are burnt white, thought Gram, he must be blind–but Peterson was grinning, his mouth drenched in blood and offal as if he were gazing into Paradise.

The sand blew up around them in a cyclone of swirling death until Peterson was left frolicking with two limp arm bones in the midst of the storm; shouting "Yes! And I always will!" as he lost his footing and staggered down the shifting sides of a dune.

Although he was bound tightly hand and foot for the long journey home, his eyes still capered gaily; two hellish white eyes dancing maniacally to a dark ancient music only he could hear.

The Brass Gong

E.W. Farnsworth

Symbol of wisdom and hieroglyph for all Egyptian prepositions, the owl sign, permeates ancient cartouches, documents, and glyphs. Uninitiated priests casually pronounced the glyph as if it were not magical. In fact, though, with each proper utterance the owl sign brought either good fortune or, more usually, misfortune to the priest and to all who heard him.

Amenhotshepsibu, who might have become Pharaoh, died of plague after pronouncing the owl glyph correctly. His consort Amenhotshepsa also died of plague, which became general, killing over one-fourth of all Egyptians. From then forward, priests purposely mispronounced the owl glyph to avoid invoking its curse. All tokens of Amenhotshepsibu's existence were purged from all public records. The only remaining records were buried with him in his minor pyramid, which was recently discovered in the Valley of the Kings. The correct pronunciation of the owl glyph and the tale of its terrible consequences remained buried for three millennia.

Recently a team of young, talented Egyptologists recreated the correct pronunciation of the owl glyph though forensic linguistics. Unaware of the curse that they were about to invoke, the precocious Egyptologists uttered the owl sign with the correct pronunciation at an international symposium in Cairo. The results of their demonstration caused a sensation. Not one attendee of that symposium survived; instead, all died of plague. The curse of Amenhotshepsibu was alive in the world again. Because the symposium was re-broadcast worldwide, plague raged globally in the name of the owl.

Of all the Egyptologists who were subjected to her colleague's pronunciation of the owl sign, only Professor Nancy Higgenbotham of the University of New Hampshire remained alive. Analysts opined that her nerve-center deafness was what saved her. Because she could speak and because she was aware of the latest forensic techniques, the 'deaf professor' was able to reconstruct and pronounce the owl sign correctly though her pronunciation had a slightly different linguistic intonation than had been offered by her colleagues at the symposium. Miraculously, her pronunciation's effects negated the effects of her colleagues' reconstruction. Her pronunciation not only stopped plague, but it also provided immunity to all diseases.

Making use of this discovery to save lives, disease control operatives destroyed all media that contained the original pronunciation of the owl sign, and then they substituted Professor Higgenbotham's pronunciation of the owl sign. As a result, the global pandemic was arrested in all regions where the Professor's intonation of the sign of the owl could be heard. The recording of her pronunciation was ordered to be administered through the PA systems of all clinics and hospitals in the world. Governments ordered that recordings of the Professor's owl sign be played at large outside events and on street corners. Commercial entrepreneurs created inexpensive recordings of the Professor's voice that could be used in universities, schools, day care centers and home nurseries. As a result, raging plague burned out and then vanished.

Ironically, the deaf professor never heard her own pronunciation of the owl sign. Nevertheless, she became a global celebrity and an instant authority on ancient curses of all kinds. Forensic intonation was said to be her broader specialty, so adventurers and tomb raiders consulted with her before they launched into the unknown.

Among those brave, lost souls was Hiram Himsely, an Oxford physical anthropologist whose passion was early hominid cave burials in southwestern China. A high mortality rate among his predecessor savants was the caution that brought Himsley to the deaf professor's door in New Hampshire that afternoon in October 2005. Higgenbotham and Himsley had communicated by encrypted email, so she was ready for their face-to-face meeting.

While Higgenbotham made tea, Himsley espied on a library table in her living room a pile of human teeth, a small sack of seeds, four round stones, and a brass gong. She brought the piping hot tea on a tray with two cups and saucers. She found her English colleague entranced by her artifacts.

"Professor, the artifacts on your table are simply remarkable," Professor Himsley said shaking his head in amazement.

"Please, it's Nancy if I may call you Hiram. Why do you find them remarkable?" She asked the question while she poured the tea and handed one cup to her colleague.

"I've found similar artifacts in each of the three cave tombs I've excavated in southwestern China. How did you come by these specimens?"

"Are you shouting, Hiram? Don't exert yourself. As long as I can see your lips, I can understand what you are saying well enough. The artifacts on the table were given to me by an explorer like yourself who was doing excavations somewhere in southwestern China in close proximity to your digs, I believe. I am not privileged to say precisely where because of a confidentiality agreement I have with the man's estate."

"So the explorer is now deceased?"

"I'm not sure. I know that he disappeared and now is presumed to be dead. Our consulting agreement novated to his estate one year after his last known contact, which was a year ago last June. I'm afraid I cannot give you details of that agreement. I brought the artifacts from the accessions room of the university museum so that you could see the kinds of things my client brought me in payment for my services. Since they were my payment, I own them. Therefore, the covenants of our agreement do not extend to them. I needed to have you confirm that the artifacts are credible because I could hardly exhibit them if they are bogus."

"I see what you mean. Quite frankly, my concern is related, I think, to your other client's concern. I have led three teams into southwestern China over the last fifteen years to do my excavations. All members of each of those three teams have died inexplicably. I am the sole survivor. How long I'm going to survive, I don't know. I want to lead a fourth team to the area next summer, but I don't want to risk their suffering the same fate as their predecessors."

"What do you need from me, Hiram?"

"I need to know what may have caused the deaths of my assistants and associates and what may prevent further deaths on my next expedition."

"I've read your publications on your digs. I know you have articles in the mill, so to speak. Tell me a little about your findings so far. I'll keep what you tell me confidential."

"May I have more tea, please? Your shortbread is excellent."

"By all means, pour yourself tea whenever you like. The shortbread is my mother's recipe. She's English. She lives in Nottingham near what's left of Sherwood Forest." Professor Himsley smiled and nodded.

"I've been working on the idea that our ancestor homo migrated from the Great Rift Valley region in Africa to southwest China much earlier than previously thought. A great many anthropologists' reputations will be shattered when the truth is finally known. The evidence I've amassed is fragmentary. Essentially, the same artifacts that lie on your table form the whole of it. The teeth are physically compelling. Carbon dating puts them at 80,000 years, give or take. The seeds may have been gathered in the hunter-gatherer fashion. The stones are ciphers. The gong is an anomaly because the Bronze Age has never been calculated as being anything like as old as the carbon dating suggests."

"I'd like to ask a question at this point. May I?"

"Of course. Please ask away."

"In all your studies of prehistoric remains, have you come across evidence that tomb hunters like yourself preceded you?"

"Often I've suspected that tomb raiders had taken priceless artifacts and left the detritus like what you have on your table. In one of the three caves in southwestern China, I found the skeleton of a woman who had harbored in the cave and died there."

"Did you find any relationship between the location of the artifacts and the orientation of the female skeleton?"

"The skeleton's right hand seemed to be holding the brass gong."

"Did you independently carbon date the gong and the skeletal remains?"

"As a matter of fact, I did. Results indicated five-thousand years plus or minus, what I'd expect for Bronze Age artifacts."

"What do you deduce from the evidence?"

"I'd say at least one and probably a team of adventurers went searching for the same caves that I've found five-thousand years ago."

"And that would account for the brass gongs you've found at every single site?"

"It would be a logical extrapolation."

"What about the four round stones on the table?"

"I found the same kind of stones in a tetrahedron configuration in each cave."

"Will you please arrange the stones on that table in that configuration?"

Professor Himsley looked closely at the four stones on the table. He then arranged three stones like a triangle and placed the fourth stone on top of the others.

"That's the way I found them."

"I'm not sure you are right, Hiram. You can see from the slanting light in this room that the orientation of the stones is not easterly as it should be. Let me realign the stones." She aligned the stones so that one base stone pointed to the east and the two adjacent stones faced west. "If I'm not mistaken, all your caves so far face east. Do they, or don't they?" She said this like a schoolmistress.

"Yes, they do. In fact, I plan to publish my ideas about these primitive hominids' superstitions about sunrise in my next article, due out this December in Physical Archaeology Review." The professor seemed very proud of his achievement, particularly now that his colleague had independently corroborated his thoughts.

"My client had similar conclusions, but he by no means thought of the hominids as primitive. He thought those early precursors of ourselves were uncannily advanced." She smiled while her hand gently caressed the four stones on the table. "Did you analyze the seeds that you found?"

"I had them analyzed by colleagues at Oxford and Cambridge. The seeds are from early specimens of edible seeds that today are considered high-energy health foods. My Oxbridge colleagues were astounded by the high protein and fat contents of the seeds."

"Did the seeds germinate?"

"It's strange that you ask that. As a matter of fact, they did germinate. The seedlings were transplanted into a special archeological garden at Balliol College,

Oxford. The plants are flourishing in a greenhouse there as I speak." He smiled and his eyes squinted. "You already knew about this?"

"Come with me into my backyard greenhouse." She stood up and walked to her back door while he followed her. In the backyard was a small greenhouse. They entered and were suddenly in a hot, humid environment. Plants luxuriated inside. An entire table of plants was labeled, "Herbs of Southwest China c. 80,000 BCE."

"I've had eighty percent germination of those seeds. That is most remarkable for seeds as old as the carbon dating implies. The seeds are not the normal seeds we associate with prehistoric hunter-gatherer diets. In fact, they are more advanced that we've discovered among the farming cultures that supposedly followed the hunter-gatherer stage of humanity." The deaf professor was reflective when she said this as if the implications of what she had imparted were profound.

"Nancy, I've been working with a number of colleagues on the DNA mutation patterns and pattern rates of hominids from 100,000 years ago to present."

"All right, Hiram, what have you found?"

"There is no way to join the DNA from the found remains to our present-day humans in that interval of time."

"What do you deduce from that?"

"Either our algorithms don't work or the carbon dating is incorrect, or both."

"My client came to the same conclusion. Let's go back inside to look at our rocks again." Nancy retraced her steps to her living room with Hiram following in her wake.

She picked up the stones one by one from the configuration and laid them in a line.

"Did you do chemical analysis on the four stones that you found in each cave?"

"I didn't do that yet. Would you advise me to do so?"

"Absolutely yes, I would. Let me give you a few hints, though. Invariably, one of the stones will be iron." She smiled while the shock set in and reflected on her colleague's face.

"Don't look so surprised. Meteorites of nearly pure iron have struck the earth for millennia. Another stone of the four will invariably be a geode. Those are the containers for beautiful, hydrated crystals of many kinds. A third stone will invariably be roseate quartz with beads of gold. The fourth stone will be filled with silver, tin and lead salts. Encapsulated, then, these four salts look forward thousands of years towards the history of metallurgy as we know it." What she said so matter-of-factly seemed to be science fiction to the Oxford professor.

"Taken together, you're suggesting that Von Danekin and his ilk are right; aliens roamed the earth."

"I'm saying nothing of the kind. I'm rather suggesting that we need more analysis of your finds to discover what they portend for your new assistants and what they mean for you."

"I've worried about my having survived when all my associates and assistants perished."

"As well you might worry. From the outside, a case might be built that you or someone else eliminated them to hide your potential findings."

"My findings are in line with other discoveries so far." He was now being defensive.

"What we've been discussing have not been part of your published work. The deductions we've made may not be publishable for hundreds of years. People are not ready for the good news. Priests and academics who hold the myths of our culture together will be outraged. They'll fight the conclusions with every means available. Some will want to kill to prevent anyone's knowing what we know. Believe me, from my experience with the Egyptian mysteries, I've found that the forces of the status quo are formidable." She said this fervently with her blue eyes glittering.

"Are you suggesting that I stop my excavations and research?" Himsley was clearly upset that his life's work might be in jeopardy.

"No, I am not. I'm just warning you that what you are about to do is dangerous to yourself and others. In your emails, you asked whether I could help you discover how to protect your assistants. Did you mean what you wrote, or not?"

"I do want to protect my expedition. The last thing I want to do is subject my people to danger and almost certain death."

"Nothing in the world can stop fate. All I can do is give you the facts that I know. I may be deaf, but my mind still works."

"Would it be improper for me to ask the last known location of your client when you lost contact with him?"

"For what it is worth, his last email arrived on Midsummer's Day in 2003. The email's contents were simple, 'You were right!'"   His previous email on the prior day gave his location as Yunnan Province, China.

"What were the contents of that earlier email?"

"He emailed that he and his team were converging on a new cave site on a yellow cliffside that locals had told him about. In response to that email, I warned him to be careful. I guess he was not careful enough."

"Be careful of what exactly?"

"I'm not sure, but in Africa hemorrhagic fever was contracted by people who had entered caves. The manner of infection was never proven, but I thought skin invasion of the virus might be caused by people not using gloves while they worked."

"The work can be hot, and gloves can get in the way sometimes."

"You mentioned that all your fellow workers died. Were there common symptoms?"

"Hemorrhagic fever may have been the common prognosis. The deaths came so swiftly that no proper diagnosis was possible. The authorities were quick to bury the corpses and hush up the circumstances."

"Well, hemorrhagic fever could link your population of hominids in China to their origin in the Rift Valley. Of course, it could also have worked in the opposite direction if the carbon dating or the theory of hominid dispersal should be incorrect. Did you follow the same protocols as your people when you went on a dig?"

"I needed to show by example what we were to do. Of course, I always followed my protocols. My people, however, did not. Perhaps that caused their unfortunate deaths?"

"We cannot be sure, but I'd advise that this time you counsel your people to follow your protocols to the letter. At the first sign of fever, engage a medical evacuation team at once and look for Marburg or some other hemorrhagic as the cause." She could see that her guest was shuddering at the thought of the effects of hemorrhagic fever.

"What you're saying is that the hominids I've found carried the disease with them. Do you think it might have caused their deaths?"

"Clinically, it might have, but then how did so many survive over such a long period? I think they knew the secret of the disease without all our modern medicine. They knew enough about it to make their burial places death traps."

"I understand what you're saying. My hominids buried their dead in caves facing east and protected the sites from intruders with a dread disease."

"Now I think you are ready to consider the brass gongs."

"What we know is that one brass gong was discovered in each of the grave sites we've found so far. Of those, one includes the skeleton of a female associated with the gong. Clearly the gong did that female no good, so the gong is not the answer to the cause of the disease."

"But the woman may have thought that the gong was the answer to whatever curse plagued the burial site. Brass was known to be a curative from its earliest manufacture. Today brass is worn to alleviate symptoms of arthritis, for example."

"I've taken your whole afternoon, Nancy, and now I'll have to go. I want to thank you for a most enlightening discussion."

"What will you do now, Hiram?"

"I'm going to China to excavate my next cave. While I'm there, I'll also try to discover what happened to your client."

"By doing that, you may just find another cave site worth investigating. But I'll warn you right now. Be careful. Follow your protocols. Come back alive. And if you come back, please bring artifacts like the ones we've played with this afternoon. Our museum could use them. More than that, they could be my recompense for having these discussions today."

Nancy showed Hiram to the door. There they shook hands. Hiram drove off in his rental car to Logan International Airport where he flew to London Heathrow International Airport. He arrived via transit to London where he had an enormous breakfast in the Automobile Club Restaurant in Mayfair with the man who wanted to fund his expedition.

"Sir Charles," Hiram said, "I'm now ready to take my new team to China if you're ready to fund the trip." He waited while his potential benefactor devoured the remains of his breakfast.

"Hiram, this is the fourth expedition I've backed, isn't it?"

"You've been most generous, Sir Charles! I could not have published my findings without your support."

"Tell me again why this fourth expedition is necessary. Your prior three expeditions have turned up the same evidence. Is a fourth not redundant?"

"It's true that we have additional work to do with the artifacts we've already found. Recently I've discovered that we need to do analytical chemistry on four rock samples we found at each site. I've also learned that we may not only have one site to investigate but also another that may have been discovered by another party."

"So you have a competitor in the field? That would be news to me. You know how I like to be funding exclusive projects. I don't know who is supporting another bloke in this line, but if it's true, I don't like it one bit."

"Think of my so-called competitor as a mere grave robber, Sir Charles. I have reliable word that whoever it is has died with all hands in his last attempt. You're well aware that all my assistants on my last three missions have died suddenly."

"So we have a curse afoot?"

"Yes, sir, I'm afraid we do."

"And you somehow survived through it all."

"Yes I did, and I'm glad to say it too."

"So how much did you say you needed again?"

"Two-hundred, fifty-thousand pounds for the expedition and ten thousand pounds for the additional chemical analysis of those rocks. I'd also like to add twenty-five thousand pounds as a medical contingency fund just in case."

"Nonsense. I'll write the bank draft right now for two-hundred-sixty thousand pounds, take it or leave it."

"I'm most grateful. Thank you." Hiram watched as his sponsor wrote the check and handed it to him.

"Here is your money. Bring back one of those brass rings for my wife especially. She rather fancied having one after I said it was all the rage in China once upon a time. Trophy wives, you know, you've got to keep them stocked with high fashion items. As for me, I'm off to the races. Maybe there I'll win back what I just gave you with the right bet. Ta ta, now. And, Himsley, please come back alive with all your crew intact." Sir Charles bolted without paying for the lunch, so the professor asked that the amount be added to the man's account with the usual gratuity. The thought of the huge gratuity brought a smile to the waiter's face.

♌♌♌

Getting his three-person team together late that evening at Oxford in his rooms, Professor Himsley led the celebration with a toast, "To the earliest hominids of southwestern China." He then launched into a briefing of what he had learned in America from the deaf professor and emphasized the protocols that, he said, would protect them all from suffering the curse that had plagued his prior expeditions.

"Herb, please run around to the assayer with these twelve samples and this order for chemical analysis of the rocks. All of you, please be ready with all your gear to fly to China next Thursday for a three-week adventure. Herb will coordinate everything for everyone. As for me, I'll be setting out three days early to scope out an additional site."

The idea of having two sites to work brought broad smiles to everyone.

Alyson said, "Two sites on one trip. That's grand! But will you be sure to meet us in China?" As a graduate intern, she was going on her first ever expedition and she was excited.

"I pledge that I'll to meet you at the foot of Xi Tang Mountain in Yunnan Province where our planned excavation is to take place on the Saturday morning after your arrival near the site. Alyson and George, do you have any questions? No? Well, get some sleep and spend a couple of days relaxing. After we start this expedition, there won't be much sleep for any of us."

Herb Grigsby was an excellent choice as Professor Himsley's second. He made sure that everything was well in hand with their team before his major professor headed for the airport.

"Have you any last moment thoughts, Professor?" Herb asked before he left Himsley at his departure gate.

"My only regret is that I couldn't get Sir Charles to agree to spend the money for an emergency medical team in case anyone had to be evacuated while we are in China."

"We'll manage somehow, sir. I've been on three other expeditions with others, as you know from my resume and references. I've seen it all, believe me. Have a great flight. We'll see you in Yunnan."

Professor Himsley had a long but uneventful flight to China. He staged in Shenzhen and flew into the outback, then rented a Jeep as ground transport to the place where his competitor last communicated with Professor Higgenbotham. Himsley inquired about him at the most likely hotel. He was informed that Professor Chumley of Clemson University in the USA had last stayed there on the night before Midsummer's Day in 2003. He had checked out and never returned. Himsley described the yellow cliff with caves, but the concierge was unable to help with that, but he summoned a local guide who would take him wherever he wanted to go.

That was how Professor Himsley made his way to the foot of the yellow cliff that the deaf professor had described during his visit. The guide told Himsley that he had led a team to a cave on the side of the cliff, but the team had not reappeared. He offered to take Himsley up to the same cave for a few thousand Yuan, which seemed a bargain. So they went up to the cave to find four skeletons in modern clothing on the cavern's floor. The guide went to inform the authorities while Himsley made a gloves-on survey of the site. First he used his cell phone to take pictures. He then harvested and placed in his knapsack four stones, a sack of seeds, a little sack full of human teeth, a bundle of threads and a brass gong.

With some satisfaction, he realized that the configuration of the stones was the same as he had seen in other such sites. With a frisson, he realized that the skeleton figure he found next to the brass gong was in the same location relative to the gong as the ancient skeleton had been at his last site. The bag of teeth was found in the right hand of the man he presumed was his competitor archeologist. A check of the man's wallet indicated that was the case.

The People's Republic of China, police and army representatives, arrived within two hours. Himsley and his guide were questioned and escorted off the site. The policeman first wanted to know how Himsley knew about the bodies in the cave. Through his guide, the professor explained how he learned about the lost expedition from a colleague in the USA. The policeman then wanted to search Himsley's knapsack, but he interdicted the attempt by showing the uniformed man the papers authorizing his participating in a dig in Yunnan. The policeman was confused by the fact that the dig noted in the paperwork was different from the current location, but the guide retorted that one permit fitted all such sites in Yunnan. The policeman did not contradict that idea though he frowned when he handed the papers back to the professor.

When Himsley and his guide made it down to the Jeep, they both breathed a sigh of relief that they were escaping the scene of a crime without a long detention.

Himsley gave his guide a tip of twice what he had offered him when they returned to the hotel. It was, he thought, the least he could do for a man who had rendered such timely service.

Then Himsley brooded on the grisly sight he had seen in the cave. He took out his cell phone and reviewed the pictures he had taken, carefully. He pulled on his gloves again to examine the artifacts he had gathered. He rationalized that he now had time to reach the hotel nearest his planned excavation site in plenty of time to meet his arriving team. In fact, he arrived there so early at his destination that he decided to reconnoiter the cave by himself.

Before he set out for the cave, though, he wrote an email to Professor Higgenbotham. He informed her of the fate of her client and attached photos he had taken as proof. She did not respond right away, but when she did respond, she inquired about artifacts. Himsley emailed that he had in his possession all the items her client's team had harvested from the site. He also wrote that he intended to bring those things to her when he returned to the U.S. The deaf professor expressed her gratitude for his having found the cave with the remains. That was the proof that the man's estate required. She would share the email with the information that the Chinese authorities could provide further substantiation of the deaths. She warned Himsley to be careful that his own team did not end up like the team he had photographed.

Professor Himsley proceeded to the cave dig site as planned. He did an initial survey and discovered some of the artifacts that he had expected to find there. The stones were configured as always and oriented towards the rising sun. The pieces of woven material were evident as was the brass gong. He did not immediately see the human teeth or the bag of seeds, but he reasoned that his team should have the pleasure of making some of the finds themselves. He took cell phone photographs of the interior of the cave.

Then he went back down to his hotel room to compose an email with attachments to Herb so he could share the information with his team. Himsley took a long, luxurious, hot shower and slept until dinner. Just before he went to dinner, he received an email from Herb acknowledging receipt of his earlier email with the pictures of the cave attached. Herb reported that he and the other team members were excited by the photos.

The next day the team arrived and met their professor. After they had a chance to check into the hotel, rest and stow their gear, everyone met for a long dinner.

"I took the opportunity to visit that other site I mentioned. I found both good news and very bad news. The good news is that the artifacts at that site confirm what I've already found at my other digs. The bad news is that I found the skeletal remains of an entire four-person team on the floor of that cave."

The team froze when they learned about the remains of the other team.

"How did they die?" asked Alyson. She was pale with apprehension and foreboding.

"Their skeletons were intact. There were no signs of shattering. My guess is that they all died of some kind of dread disease. It must have been very fast-acting because the bodies were laid out on the cool cave floor almost as if they had died instantly."

"The cave was cursed," Alyson said in a tremulous tone. "Maybe we shouldn't be going up to our cave in the morning."

"Come on, Alyson. Don't get weak-kneed now that we're so close," said Herb trying to show some leadership.

"Professor Himsley, what do you think are the risks?" asked George, always the practical one.

"George, I don't know what to tell you. I went into that other cave and came out alive. I also went up to our cave. In both cases, I wore the gloves that I mandated for the team's use. I picked up the artifacts from the other cave, but I left the artifacts at the Yi Tang site so you could see them exactly as they are without modern human interference. From the evidence, the odds are one in three that you'll come out alive if you count my guide to the other site."

"The prof has proven we can do this thing."

"Yes, but I used the protocols exactly as I trained you to do. I make no guarantees for anyone not following the guidelines explicitly."

Alyson was the only team member who still had doubts.

The next morning before the team had a chance to gather for breakfast, Chinese police, and army representatives arrived at the hotel and asked to see Professor Himsley. Through their own interpreter, they informed him that the guide who had shown him the way to the cave had died suddenly. The combined police and army team that was trying to remove the remains of the tomb raiders at the other site had all died as well of mysterious circumstances. The reason they had come to Himsley was to be sure he was all right. They said they fully expected to find that he had expired. They apologized for having inconvenienced Himsley and went away.

At breakfast, Himsley told his team what had happened. He told his team that he had made a command decision; they would use his photography from both caves and the artifacts he had gleaned from the other cave to satisfy the requirements of their expedition. That having been done, he said their expedition was over. He ordered Herb to arrange for transportation back to England as soon as possible. The team members were both upset at having been denied their dig and relieved that they were not going to be subjected to danger and possibly even death. Alyson was the only one who really took umbrage with the professor's decision.

"Professor, we've all come a very long way to work with you on this dig. Here we are in Yunnan within walking distance of our objective. You've already been there and scouted it out. You even took pictures. How tantalizing! Now we're supposed to pack up again and return to Oxford like the King of France and his forty-thousand men marching up the hill and marching down again? I for one am not going to cut and run. I came for a reason—and my resume, and I'll not go back until I've accomplished my mission. I'll go up the hill alone if I have to. But first I'm going to have my breakfast."

"Alyson, I understand your frustration. You saw how serious the Chinese were about what has happened. You'll get your credit and your name will be included in any articles that stem from what we have done. Will that satisfy you? At least let's talk about this over breakfast."

So the team had breakfast, and the professor had a split decision by the end of the meal. Alyson's arguments had appealed to George, but not to Herb. So it was the professor and his second hand against the others. The professor offered a compromise to break the tie. He said that he would take Alyson and George to the site and let them take cell phone pictures with their gloves on. His proviso was that neither should take off the gloves or touch anything sharp in the cave. Herb was not to enter the cave but remain outside in case of trouble. While Alyson still protested that she wanted to get her hands dirty rummaging for teeth on the floor of the cave, she knew that she would be overruled. She backed down and acceded to the professor's final deal.

The group went to the cave. Herb stood guard outside while the professor, Alyson and George went inside with their gloves on and their cell phone cameras out. After fifteen minutes, they reemerged from the cave with their pictures. The professor had gathered the visible artifacts in his knapsack. They lacked only the teeth, but Himsley decided he must have the teeth. So he handed his knapsack to Alyson and told her and George to go back down the hill. He told Herb to wait outside the cave until he had gathered the teeth. Then he went inside the cave again with a handkerchief tied over his nose and mouth and a dibble in his right hand. His intention was to scour the surface of the cave's floor for the missing teeth.

Himsley worked for an hour scraping the floor carefully and using his cell phone torch to view what he had unearthed. He could not find a single tooth. This he thought odd. In every other cave he had found, including the one where the four bodies had been found, teeth were the prizes. They definitively proved that the sites had been used by hominids. After another hour of delicately scraping around the edges of the interior of the cave, Himsley decided that he had done enough to prove that the teeth were not inside. He figured that negative information was still information, so he backed out of the cave. There he met Herb, who was glad that his professor was still alive. They proceeded back down the hill to their hotel where Himsley discarded his gloves and kerchief. He asked all his team to take soapy showers to be sure that they had not come in contact with viridian materials.

When everyone had showered and changed clothing, Himsley hosted a triumphant dinner. The team had, he said, done their explorations and had in their possession the only artifacts that were available. On a side table, he ranged the stones, the brass gongs, the sack of teeth and the sacks of seeds. Over wine, he lectured on the deductions that he and Professor Higgenbotham had made during his trip to New

Hampshire. He also told his assistants about the chemical analysis he had ordered before he left England.

Alyson was intrigued by the thought that some deadly virus protected each of the cave burial sites. Himsley told her that protecting burial sites with chemical and biological agents was as old as time. In ancient Egypt, for example, the tombs of the pharaohs had been protected by agents that scientists were still trying to decipher today.

"I can understand chemical agents because they serve to kill anyone daring to enter and rob from the tombs. I don't understand the biological agent because it could cause widespread destruction well beyond the tomb."

"Consider Herb, that this biological agent is a deadly virus that kills almost immediately. Think of the four bodies on the floor of that other cave. It must have worked faster than the most lethal viruses known to contemporary man. It is a virus that acts exactly like a lethal chemical agent."

"Professor, that's frightening."

"That's why I was reluctant to subject you to that virus today. I'm hoping that you will not succumb to it as I have not."

"Can you think of any reason why you did not catch the virus when all your other team members died of it?" asked George.

"No, I cannot. Perhaps I am immune. Perhaps the hominids whose teeth we found were also immune, but I somehow doubt it."

"Professor Himsley, isn't it true that the hominids at one point defeated the Neanderthals throughout what is now Europe?"

"That's the prevailing theory, yes."

"So is it possible that this virus caused the deaths of those Neanderthals and let the hominids live?"

"If we are related to the hominids you are talking about, they would have died along with their enemies. Consider the deaths of the many excavators including those from my prior teams."

"One other thing I'm curious about is the implication of the brass gongs."

"Okay, Herb, what do you make of those?"

"They imply that we are not the first to explore these cave burials. Your finding a Bronze Age female holding a brass gong indicates that. So before the time of the first pyramids in Egypt teams just like ours were scouring the countryside for burial sites that hark back to the beginnings of mankind."

"Go on."

"Well, for seventy-five thousand years no one cared. Then suddenly someone cared enough to manufacture countless brass gongs and put one in every burial cave that was found. In at least one case, that caused the death of the explorer."

"At least they made a positive contribution to the burial site."

"How so?"

"They left the brass gongs."

"I see what you mean. We, in contrast, take everything and leave nothing."

"In the case of the other cave that we will definitely not be visiting as a group, if I had not decided to check out what happened to our competitors, all four bodies and what they were wearing would have remained at the site for as long as it took for the next enterprising generation to go looking for those caves again. In fact, how many expeditions have been undertaken to find those caves will not be known until all the caves are found."

"The way some American Indian burials sites were formed in large earthen shapes, we might be searching for a long time to find all those sites." This was Herb's hopeful announcement.

"Yes. That's why we need archeologists like you three. If you made it your mission in life to find and map the other sites, we might begin to know the mysteries we have uncovered today."

"Are you ready to go back to Oxford and write up what we've found?" the professor queried his team.

"We have enough information to satisfy our course requirements, I suppose," said Alyson.

"Teamed with the professor, we have a lot more than that," said Herb.

"Wait a minute!" interposed George, "We're forgetting something really important."

"What's that, George?" Alyson asked, bored and ready to move right on.

"This virus is pretty deadly."

"Definitely, it is."

"And it could kill a lot of innocent people as well as a lot of grave robbers."

"Go on. Make your point."

"What is to prohibit the Chinese from discovering what this virus is and weaponizing it?"

"That's nonsense," Alyson quipped.

"No, Alyson, that's genius," the professor exclaimed. "That's another reason we're all going to pack our things tonight and depart the first thing tomorrow morning. Herb, make the arrangements tonight, please." The professor had an alarmed look in his eyes. He was anxious to be on the move. Like an infection, his team members caught his excitement without being able to penetrate the source.

The next morning the four made their way out of China and flew back to England without incident. When they arrived in Oxford, they settled back into their scholarly routine.

Professor Himsley briefed Sir George about their expedition and discussed what needed to happen next for planning purposes. The professor was always selling the next expedition, and he was pleased to report that everyone had returned safely from the last one.

He gave Sir George the brass gong he had promised to bring for the great man's trophy wife. Sir George almost jumped out of his seat for joy when he received it. The brass gong, having been polished to a sheen, was gorgeous. Sir George said he would build a mount for it as a setting. He was so happy that the professor decided to ask him right then for another twenty-five thousand pounds for his next dig. The man wrote the bank order immediately, and once again he left the table without settling the bill for the quail and canard, the fine wine and the liquor. Himsley told the waiter to place the cost of the meal with a large gratuity on the great man's account. Everyone was pleased at the lunch, including the Automobile Association.

ฌฌฌ

At Christmas break, Himsley flew back to New Hampshire to talk with the deaf professor, who was glad to see him again. He turned over the artifacts that he had harvested from the cave where the four bodies had been found. She watched as he laid them on her table, glad that he remembered how to stack the stones. She was particularly interested in the brass gong. She asked Himsley to see what she had made of the other gong that she had shown him on his previous visit. Like the gong he had presented to Sir George, this gong was burnished to a sheen. Professor Higgenbotham had mounted it as a gong should be mounted and equipped it with a baton so that it could be struck. She handed Himsley the baton.

"Hiram, strike the gong, please. Don't be bashful."

So Hiram Himsley struck the gong and heard its resonating tone. Happy with the sound, he struck it again and again.

"Nancy, its tone is spell-bindingly beautiful."

"Yes, it is. You may recall we discussed many possibilities for this gong having been deposited in the caves where the burials had taken place, but we never talked about the meaning of the tones these gongs make when struck." She smiled as it dawned on her friend what she was suggesting.

"Tell me, Nancy, what does the tone do?" He leaned closer to her so he could hear her clearly after his ears had been affected by the gong.

"I believe that the gong is the antidote to the horrible virus that infects the caves you've been exploring. Don't ask me how it happens. I'm no virologist."

"I think I understand you, but let me ask a couple of questions to be sure."

"Fire away, Hiram."

"Are you suggesting that the Bronze Age intruders knew that the curse of the graves had something to do with an invisible death-dealing cause and used the gongs as the antidote?"

"They knew nothing about viruses, but they knew about cause and effect."

"Why would they have been left in the caves?"

"Let's assume that they were left to help any who found them survive the effects of having entered the caves."

"That means that unaccountable deaths had occurred in such numbers that as with our improvised explosive devices, the authorities found it more cost effective to spend on a known antidote than to find the cause of the deaths and remove it?"

"I'd say that's close enough for this Christmas season, wouldn't you?"

"But one female had a gong but died anyway."

"Proving nothing but that the poor fool did not know how to use what she had."

"I take it that you mounted this gong as an antidote, then."

"I did, and I've not had a single cold this year. That's a first."

"After our celebration, I must get back to tell my team in England about this. But I also must raise the question that one of my assistants brilliantly posed to me."

"Let me guess, what are we going to do about the possibility of weaponizing the virus for use in war?"

"Precisely. How did you know?"

"I was contacted by the authorities from a place called the United States Army Research Institute for Infectious Diseases. They were most serious gentlemen in uniform. They asked all about my connection to that unfortunate professor and his team whom you found in that cave in Yunnan, China. They wanted to know many more details than I could possibly know as a forensic anthropologist. Anyway, you should stand warned that your Porton Downs folks are likely to be calling on you soon to ask the same questions. So will you have some of my English Plum Pudding with freshly whipped cream? I'll take that for a yes."

After the friends had spent a quiet weekend together, Himsley returned to Oxford where he immediately arranged to have his gong polished and mounted with a baton. He also had lunch with Sir George and told the great man the medicinal benefits of the brass gong. The knight grumbled about how difficult it was to keep a trophy wife happy. It seems they were getting a divorce. He said he would mount the polished gong on his country estate by the stables.

"The damned thoroughbreds are always coming down with something. This might do nicely to help with that. By the bye, the boys from Porton Downs dropped by to talk about some virus rubbish you diddled with in China. They were most importunate, I thought. Anyway, they'll be visiting you in your digs in Oxford sometime soon. I'd make time to see them, if I was you. What have you gotten me into this time, Himsley? Well, no matter, I'm off to the hounds this weekend. Just sit here and enjoy your port wine. Leave when you like. And have them put the whole bill against my account."

Professor Hiram Himsley sat back in his plush leather seat at the Automobile Club Restaurant. He enjoyed his seventeen-year-old port to the last drop. He mused about the mystery of the brass gong. He already had in his own account the money for his next expedition. Should he return to China to find yet another hominid cave burial? He thought he might look into the new Indian finds in Belize. At least, he thought as he waved to the waiter, those ruins had not been overrun by enthusiasts from the Bronze Age. How could they have been when they were only constructed two millennia later?

The Curse of Nilofer

Rekha Ambardar

Noted Egyptologist, Miles Cramer, ran his hand lightly over the dusty veneer of the three-thousand-year-old wooden sarcophagus, trying to read the disjointed hieroglyphics on it. Miles and photographer, Ajib Anwar of the Supreme Council of Egyptian Antiquities were in the tomb of a long-dead queen, who to all purposes was banished and dishonored by her people millennia ago.

"A pathetic end to an illustrious life," Miles said to Ajib. "Queen and consort to Pharaoh Smenkare of the 18th Dynasty, buried in an ordinary wooden sarcophagus without pomp or splendor. Why?"

"Perhaps the hieroglyphics on the sarcophagus will tell us why," Ajib suggested.

Bats whizzed around them as the two men peered at the faded markings etched on the ancient wood. Ajib held up a large strobe light for them to see better in the dingy gloom of the tomb. Several of these winged, nocturnal creatures clung to the sharp, rocky edges inside the makeshift mausoleum. If the men were lucky, the more indolent of them would not zigzag around them, and would leave them to their task.

The temperature in the tomb soared to well over a hundred degrees Fahrenheit by Miles's estimation. Sweat poured down the faces of both men as Miles ran his hand over the markings. Despite the intense heat and the vile, musty odor the men concentrated on the sarcophagus.

"The hieroglyphics show that Queen Nilofer was banished during the twelfth year of Smenkare's reign," the Egyptologist muttered, straining his eyes to study the etchings despite the glare of the strobe light.

"A queen banished? Impossible." Ajib said. "For what reason?"

Miles didn't reply. He concentrated on the figures etched on the sarcophagus and started muttering again. "It shows the figures of a man and a woman together–Nilofer and this man. Apparently she betrayed the Pharaoh with this man–so the hieroglyphs say. Perhaps adultery. It also says here she was beloved by her husband and she shamed him. He did not have it in his heart to have her executed," Miles said. He took out a soiled handkerchief from his safari shirt pocket and wiped his face.

"So the Pharaoh banished her," Ajib said, setting the heavy light on a sand-whipped rock that jutted out from the wall.

"Not only that," Miles said. "She probably perished in the desert from heat and starvation." He sat back on his haunches in the sand that constituted the floor of the tomb.

"You notice this tomb is at a distance from the Valley of the Kings where all the pharaohs and consorts are buried," Miles said. "Nilofer brought dishonor to the Pharaoh and his court so she was given the burial of a pauper." He glanced around at the paraphernalia of the after-life–stools, plates, barley, drinking cups, clothing–but these were items that not even the poorest peasant would claim to own, pitiable trash thrown at a mendicant.

Ajib set up a tripod and placed a titanic-sized piece of equipment, a state-of-the-art camera that could easily double up as an AK 45, and he started clicking noisily. The noisier the camera, the more cutting edge, Miles thought with a wry grin as he glanced up briefly.

Miles painstakingly ran a small brush over the hieroglyphics in short, deft strokes, trying to remove the dust of millennia.

An hour went by as each man concentrated on his task. Then Miles opened the sarcophagus and studied the mummy again. Its arms were crossed over the chest in the position depicting royalty. The palm of the right hand held what looked like a piece of ancient cloth.

Miles gently extracted the cloth from the palm of the mummy through a hole near the wrist. Nilofer's mummy was not in the best state of preservation. Miles placed the cloth and seeds in a plastic bag he pulled out from his pocket. What seeds were they and who had put them in her hand, as if to accompany her in her journey through eternity? He'd have to examine the seeds and see if he could identify them. They could provide a clue to understanding this enigmatic woman.

Ajib had stopped clicking and was putting away the equipment in heavy-duty carrying cases. He turned toward Miles, who contemplated the seeds.

"What do you have in your hand?" Ajib asked Miles.

"Seeds of some sort," Miles said. "I want to take them back and figure out what they are."

Ajib scrutinized them as they lay in Miles' palm.

"They look like coffee beans, smooth and dark brown," Ajib said shining the strobe light on them.

Miles nodded, then looked around at the dismal disarray of the tomb and felt pity for the woman buried in it.

"We'd better get out of here," Miles said. "We'll be back tomorrow." He shouldered the canvas bags containing his notes and brushes. "Remember not to talk to reporters. All we say is that we found a tomb belonging to an unknown queen."

"Okay," Ajib said and hefted his equipment out of the crawl space in the tomb with Miles following at his heels.

Outside the harsh, white glare of the sun beat down on them, causing them to squint. Miles put on his shades and cap. The red bandana around his neck was now soaking wet. He removed it and stuffed it in a side pocket of his carryall. He patted the plastic bag with the seeds in it lying safely in his shirt pocket.

Back at the hotel, Miles took a closer look at the seeds and then consulted a source book on rare plants of Africa. Despite pouring over it for over an hour, none of the plants and seeds he scanned looked like the seeds he held in his hand.

Tired from leafing through the sourcebook and scrolling through pages on his laptop, he pulled away from the desk in his hotel room and threw himself on the bed, dusty boots and all,

His eyes had been watery all day—from the glare of the strobe light or from concentrating too hard on the etchings, he didn't know. He closed them now and felt himself drift away into waves of sleep. But it was a fitful sleep, earning him no rest.

Strange images arrested him as he lay there. He saw a large, cavernous hall where priests were bent over a macabre task–of mummifying a corpse. Huge canopic jars stood nearby awaiting the organs of the deceased. He couldn't see who the mummy was. One of the priests squatted on the floor consulting the Book of the Dead, the handbook for rules to guide the deceased through eternity.

Suddenly the corpse arose and lunged toward Miles, but he still couldn't see its face. A gaping hole showed where the face should have been.

Milles awoke in a cold sweat, and sat up, his heart thudding in his chest. He didn't know what to make of the images that had so startled him. The wraith of the vicious creature that had lunged at him seemed like a mummy, but somehow it didn't seem like the mummy of Nilofer. There was something uncouth and gargantuan about this one.

He shook his head and looked around the room taking comfort from the common everyday things in it. His backpack of notes and manuals, his laptop, a functional digital camera, bottles of drinking water, the small refrigerator that the hotel thankfully provided.

Miles spent the rest of the afternoon pouring over his notes, still trying to identify the seeds. No luck.

A call from his wife, Elaine, in Pennsylvania, broke the tedium of the day. She missed him and when was he coming home? In a couple of weeks, he told her. She'd understood that he'd have to travel when they got married three years ago. Forty years old was late for a guy to get married, but his work was as demanding as a spouse, and Elaine competed with his work sometimes, much to his wry sense of irony. Sometimes she'd accompany him, but not often. She was the owner of a boutique in Philadelphia and she couldn't leave her work.

He glanced at the seeds on the table. Were they shrinking in size or was he still in the grip of the bad dream?

Elaine's phone call left him both homesick and desperate to finish his quest of identifying Nilofer's history. He'd then turn over the excavation to the Egyptian Supreme Council of Antiquities and head home to Pennsylvania, back to teaching in the archeology department at the university.

The next day, all hell broke loose. The media, both Egyptian, and U.S. got wind of the excavation and demanded to know who the mystery mummy in the tomb was. Was there a mummy? Or was this hype perpetrated by the Egyptian Antiquities Authority and the archeologist from America?

Ajib joined Miles at the hotel to go over the day's excavation activities, and Miles told him about the furor that broke over the discovery of the mummy of Nilofer, and the demand to know the veracity of the news.

"I could show them the photos I took yesterday to let them know that we indeed have a discovery," Ajib said, setting the heavy equipment on the hotel room floor, then he open the cases one by one and set the lenses on the table. Obviously, he was on a mission to set the media straight about the excavation even though he and Ajib didn't need to convince anybody about anything, just bring the valuable find to light and give it the recognition it deserved.

Ajib rolled his shoulders to relieve the soreness of carrying the equipment and then proceeded to look for the pictures he had taken.

"Releasing the pictures before we catalog the finds is premature," Miles said cautiously. Ajib was liable to get hot-headed if crossed, and he didn't particularly like Doubting Thomases. "We need the time to get details of the artifacts and catalog them before releasing them to the Antiquities Authority, and then we leave with our reputations intact."

Ajib's shoulders went slack and he seemed to relent–for now. "Did you find out about the seeds? What are they?" he asked peering at them at close quarters.

"Not yet." Miles got up from the table. "I just need to find the right source book of rare plants." He blinked. The glare from being out in the boiling sun at the dig hadn't quite left his eyes. It was as if it were following him around–an in-your-face searchlight, the penalty for disturbing the dead queen. He didn't believe any of that malarkey anyway, still was there a germ of truth in it somewhere?

Miles shook his head. The blinding haze held him captive and he had more work to do. He had made a major discovery and he had to keep going with it.

Ajib sat at the table and started fidgeting with his camera. Miles strained to look over Ajib's shoulder. Ajib pushed the notch to 'Display' to view the pictures he'd taken at the tomb, and waited. Nothing–as in no pictures. Just a blank where the pictures should have been.

Miles frowned. "I thought I heard you clicking away. Where are the pictures?" he asked.

"I don't know. I only know I took a lot of pictures," Ajib said, his face drawn and his forehead etched with worry lines. "What has happened to them?"

Miles shook his head. He could offer no explanations either. Ancient mummy curses were too corny to believe in this day and age. But where were the pictures?

"You didn't delete them by mistake, did you?" Miles asked, then regretted it. Ajib was the poster boy for professionalism. Carelessness was not something you ascribed to his mode of operation.

"No. I created a file just for these pictures so they wouldn't get lost," Ajib said. He laid the camera back on the table and wiped his face with a large, cotton handkerchief.

"Well, we're going back there early tomorrow. You can take more pictures," Miles said.

Ajib seemed somewhat shaken by the disappearance of the pictures he had so painstakingly amassed. He didn't say much but stared glassily at his camera equipment as if he believed it had betrayed him somehow.

Early next morning saw both Miles and Ajib at the excavation site. Armed with equipment and bottles of lukewarm water, they crawled into the cavernous hole that even a beggar wouldn't call home.

The sarcophagus stood waiting for them in the dark, dusty corner where it had sat for millennia.

Miles set his bags down on the sandy floor of the tomb and took out his brushes. He bent over the sarcophagus and started brushing away the dust from its patina as delicately as possible using the finest of brushes from his collection. It was as if he didn't want to disturb the mummy's repose, but it was his life's mission to bring the artifact to light.

The mask on the sarcophagus had intrigued him from the day they had discovered the tomb, but today there was a change in–what was it–the expression of the face? It showed a slight distortion in its mien–almost a look of utter disdain. The face distended into a rictus, a self-contented sneer as if its owner knew something denied to Miles and his cohort.

The two men stared at it dumbfounded.

"The mask," Miles said in a hoarse whisper. "It looks different. Do you see it?" He was too aghast to sift through all the possible causes, one of which may be that they just didn't notice it before being busy with cleaning away the debris surrounding the sarcophagus.

"It looks insane," Ajib said. In the eerie glow of the strobe light he carried, the tomb and the mask looked surreal.

Miles couldn't make any sense of it. For the first time, he wanted to finish the excavation, hand over the sarcophagus to the Antiquities Council and go home.

Ajib started setting up his camera equipment.

"You're going to try taking pictures again?" Miles asked, looking up from the wooden paneling of the sarcophagus.

"Yes–again. Let's see what happens this time. Maybe I deleted the pictures by mistake." Obviously Ajib was beginning to doubt his professional prowess.

Miles took out a sketchbook and started to pictorially document the items in the near vicinity of the sarcophagus–potsherds, faience beads of no general color, drinking mugs, and small stools. He used a whole page to sketch the sarcophagus with the mask, now grotesque in its grinning repose. How would he explain this to the Antiquities Council? Miles was sounding his death knell by submitting a drawing of this. But if the pictures that Ajib was so laboriously taking didn't show up again, they'd need some evidence and cataloging of their discoveries. The only thing he didn't document were the seeds. These he intended to keep for himself.

Four miserable, sweltering hours later, working in above a hundred-degree heat, with sweat pouring down their foreheads, the men finished up their work. It was too difficult to continue. Miles's eyes felt watery and hazy again. He was concentrating too hard on the drawings. Enough was enough.

He had spent months at the site trying to identify the mummy, and he had finally succeeded. It was time to leave in more ways than one.

Ajib had stopped clicking.

"Check the pictures before we leave," Miles said.

Ajib clicked on 'Display'. Nothing.

"No pictures," Ajib said, his voice cracking. "I don't understand it." He put down the camera and hit his fist against the red, sandy wall of the tomb.

"Take it easy. There must be some rational explanation," Miles said. "Maybe the intense heat somehow wipes out everything on the camera." Miles tried not to reveal his own agitation. "In any case, I've got drawings of the artifacts. We'll submit copies of them." It wasn't like Ajib to put his fist through the wall. He was usually placid and meticulous.

ฦ ฦ ฦ

Dr. Hadi Mahmood, Director of the Antiquities Council, a rotund and volatile man, jumped in apoplexy when informed that no photos of the newly-discovered tomb had materialized.

Miles and Ajib were in the holding area for new artifacts at the Cairo Museum where the workers had trucked in the sarcophagus and the supporting items carefully from the excavation site.

"What do you mean no photos?" Mahmood roared, his large belly undulating like waves on the ocean. "They have to be sent to the media." He turned to Ajib. "You could have requisitioned one of our freelance photographers," he bellowed.

"We understand, Hadi," Miles said calmly, "but something happened. The pictures just didn't show up. There were at least a hundred."

"Photos just don't disappear," Mahmood said looking like a gorilla deprived of his noonday snack in the wilds.

"The heat and the humidity at the site could have destroyed them," Miles said.

"What? You can't believe that?" If Mahmood got any angrier he'd have a stroke, Miles thought.

"I have sketches of them," Miles said and handed them over.

Mahmood shook his head as he took them from Miles with a flourish. "The mummy is safe at least," he said finally. He didn't say anything about the grotesque expression on the face. Mahmood hadn't seen the sarcophagus before the facial expression changed so he wouldn't know the difference, Miles figured.

Miles filed the necessary papers with the artifacts, identifying each of them except the seeds. He was going to plant them in a pot when he got home.

𝄞 𝄞 𝄞

Miles let himself into their ranch-style home. It was a sweltering day and someone sure had neglected to turn on the air. He dumped his bags in the hallway and went looking for Elaine. He'd emailed her–she should've been somewhere in the vicinity welcoming him home. He'd told her he'd be home soon, hadn't he?

He kicked off his sneakers and padded around in his socks looking for Elaine. Looking for Elaine–he grinned wryly. If that wasn't a metaphor! Had he really ever discovered her?

He trudged into the bedroom. The closets were open and all of Elaine's clothes gone. There were two suitcases also missing–hers.

He called her cell phone. Her somber voice greeted him. He left a message, "Elaine, I'm home. Where are you?"

That done, he brought his bags into the bedroom and then peeked into the den. The PC stood on the desk waiting to be turned on, but he wasn't going that route. Enough work. He wanted his life back, and Elaine too, if she was around somewhere.

Miles decided to fix himself something to eat. He found cold cuts, wheat bread, mustard, mayo, and a carton of milk in the refrigerator. Elaine had thoughtfully left some staples. He poured himself a glass of milk and slapped together a sandwich and munched on it.

He felt much better after his snack. But something was missing. The air. He turned on the system and threw himself on the vinyl sofa in the den.

He must have dozed off. When he awoke, he groggily saw someone standing in front of him.

"Elaine! Where've you been?" Miles said struggling to sit up.

"Moving my things, Miles," she said quietly. "I'm leaving you."

He shook his head as if he was still trying hard to wake up. "Well, this is some homecoming," he said.

"If you only knew how lonely it's been these many years," Elaine said.

"Without so much as a discussion?"

"You were never around to talk," she said reproachfully.

"We can talk now," Miles said. "I'm home."

"It's too late, Miles. Maybe someday you'll understand."

He was too tired to argue or fight what was coming. "Well, if that's the way you want it, Elaine. Where are you moving too?"

"An apartment."

"Is there someone else?" Miles held his breath.

"Yes, there is."

Miles didn't want to know who it was. If Elaine was leaving, so be it. All he wanted was to get some sleep, for days. Then maybe his head would clear so he could think clearly.

Elaine disappeared as suddenly as she had appeared in front of him, obviously not at all bothered by remorse for leaving.

His hand went to his head, it hurt too much to cajole her into reconsidering her decision. Besides, it wouldn't work anyway.

After she had left, Miles fell back on the sofa and drowned himself in sleep again. This time, he was ambushed by the nightmare of the headless mummy lunging at him.

He was suddenly jogged out of his sleep, not knowing where he was for a moment. He could have sworn he was at the mummy's tomb. His face and body broke into a sweat and his head hurt even more than before. A shower—a cool shower—that's what he needed.

Miles peeled off the sweaty clothes he'd worn for two days and savored the flow of cool water cascading over him.

An hour later, feeling better, he unpacked his bags. He found the seeds and laid them on the table in his bedroom. Tomorrow he'd find a pot and plant them and see what came up.

ॐ ॐ ॐ

It was several days before he found a planter in the shed and bought potting soil to plant the seeds. He then took it to the den and set it by the window where the sunlight poured in.

More days flew by. Days filled with writing reports on the excavation site, replying to emails from Dr. Mahmood in Cairo. Mahmood seemed pleased with the press that the discovery was getting. *It's all yours,* Miles thought, *take all the credit. I want no part of it.*

It must have been because his own life was spiraling downward or maybe the sarcophagus seemed so baffling that nothing seemed explicable. At least Ajib was as normal as can be. Or was he?

Ajib's last email sounded like the ramblings of a mad man. "I can't sleep. Something churns in my throat," the first email read. "Somebody is poisoning my food–it's Nilofer or is it my wife? We are living with my wife's relatives now as we need help."

None of it made sense to Miles. Ajib was the nicest guy he had worked with–and the sanest.

Elaine came and went. Sometimes she was accompanied by Roger, her new boyfriend, a big oaf of a fellow, who seemed to have all the time in the world to work out in the gym, judging by his biceps.

"Hello, Miles," she said one morning, letting herself in with her key. "I want you to meet Roger."

He shook hands with the guy in as civil a manner as Miles could summon even though he wanted to belt Roger and knock the smug look on his face.

Elaine looked around the living room, at the scattered papers and plate of half-eaten breakfast. "The place could use cleaning." Then she peered at Miles. She was short-sighted and refused to get glasses. "Are you eating okay?"

Miles didn't answer that. "Well, are you here to pick up more of your things?" he asked, wanting them out of his house as soon as possible.

"Yes. Roger's helping me."

"Okay." Miles went back to his papers. The mummy was soon to be displayed in Cairo, the U.S. and Canada, and Mahmood had sent Miles the details of the tour and the promotions.

Elaine and her boyfriend left after an hour or so of back-and-forthing and Miles hoped never to see Elaine again except through a lawyer.

ℓℓℓ

Two months went by and Miles got ready for another excavation. This time to the Sudan where a remote and forgotten tribe had established its civilization, only to disappear mysteriously after a thousand years.

One day when he was in the den he noticed that the plant had grown to a height of one foot, and small white blossoms were starting to push through. He stared at it dumbfounded. He hadn't expected the seeds to germinate. He had to find out what the plant was.

As the flowers blossomed, they sent out a strong but pleasant fragrance and it somehow fascinated Miles. He had never known of any ancient seeds that grew into a plant, and he kept a close watch on the plant.

He didn't know if it was the strain of preparing for the new expedition or the weather that made him drowsy and tired each day. He felt worse by the day, but he didn't want to see a doctor. He couldn't afford to slow down now.

Miles slept on the sofa in the den to be near the plant that fascinated him so much. But he could barely lift himself out of the sofa in the morning. He finally called Elaine.

Elaine took one look at him and said she was calling the doctor. "I'm worried," she said, her forehead furrowing.

"I'll be okay."

"No heroics now." She called the doctor and took Miles to see him.

"Just a flu bug," he said.

"In summer?"

"Sometimes it can happen," the doctor said and sent him home with a prescription and an order to rest and a lot of fluids.

A week later, Miles found what he was looking for in one of the electronic databases of the university library. He'd forced himself to drive there and spent three hours on the computer, making his eyes ache more than ever. The plant was of East African origin and was called Adenia Volkensii, passion flower, and contained a cyanogenic glycoside and a phytotoxin, and the blossoms resembled a cobra hood. Some African tribes used this poison as hyena bait.

Miles's fascination with the plant grew more intense. He rummaged among his notes to look for the pictographs of the hieroglyphics he had drawn so carefully.

The pictures told him more of what he wanted to know. He had missed it before in his hurry to race against the soaring temperature in the tomb.

Nilofer was depicted as trying to poison the pharaoh Smenkare with the help of her lover, using the insidious plant–and she had nearly succeeded until the Pharaoh discovered the plot and banished her into the desert–and certain death. The seeds had been placed in her hand as a testimony to her treason against the Pharaoh.

Miles blinked as he threw the pictographs back into the pile and dragged himself back to the sofa. What evil had compelled Nilofer to orchestrate her doomed plot?

He hoisted himself up and took the potted plant into the kitchen and pulled it out, shook it free of the sod and dumped it into the trash compacter.

That done, he lay on the living room sofa. The overpowering fragrance now penetrated the entire house. He took out his cell phone and dialed Elaine. He left a message, "Elaine, come as soon as possible."

ᐁᐁᐁ

Elaine opened the door and found Miles unconscious. She tried his pulse, but couldn't feel anything so she called the ER at the hospital.

Roger came in the front door, "What happened?"

"I don't know, but I'm worried," Elaine said almost in a whisper. "These expeditions have killed him. I was afraid something like this would happen." She sniffed the air. "What's that smell?"

"Probably air freshener," Roger said.

They went into the den and found a pile of drawings and papers. "I don't know what all this means," Elaine said sadly.

Back in the living room she sat on the edge of the sofa. "I'm selling this house. Poor Miles." Her voice faded and her eyes pricked with tears as they waited…

The Dead King's Bones

Matthew Wilson

Richal raised the spear and entered the sacred tomb first. The king had only been dead for two weeks but with how much the old tyrant was hated, Richal wouldn't be surprised if braver grave robbers burned the place–treasures and all for the curse lain upon them.

Richal couldn't afford to be superstitious, he'd prayed for great things from the goddess and for his efforts, she had killed his mom with TB and withered dad's crops. If he remained law abiding, then he'd be dead within a month.

Dad had been a fool to believe the tyrants lie and join his army. Yes, there would be riches enough to ensure his two sons grew fat like no other children on the Nile shores. But dad was long dead since a poison tipped arrow pierced his neck on a distant battlefield.

Now Richal and his brother, Soran had to do what was necessary–not what was right–to survive.

"Gods, it smells in here," Richal tried his best not to step on sleeping rodents that had burrowed in here to escape the cold. "Don't look at the walls," Richal had promised mom on her deathbed that he would look after his brother and it was a good thing the wannabe thief couldn't read the curses plastered here, but the severed bodies of trapped criminals were a picture worth a thousand nightmares.

"Stay close," Richal hissed, trying to breathe through his mouth now the foul juices used to keep the tyrant forever youthful in his coffin had soured in the heat.

King Arat had never been loved, but as a youth had known that whenever he felt sad, he only had to kill a few servants to feel better. No one complained, not after Arat slit his sleeping father's throat and took his crown for his own.

Arat felt a show of force would deter other heroes to take him down too. Through thirty countries, he'd led his army, burning all towns so none could grow strong enough to rise up against him. Men dying of starvation could not wield a spear.

The people feared him but by his fiftieth year, Arat was bored with conquering, certain that the history pages would forever hold his name; he returned home to Cairo and found something wonderful had happened.

His brother, Odat had long been banished for whispering rebellion, and the last time they had met by chance at market, breathless after the long chase, Odat had managed to stab his brother in the leg before leaping in the Nile. King Arat had thought him drowned, but when he returned home with great pomp and ceremony, he thought it splendid that his brother had come out from under the rocks at last.

Arat had been away for years and thousands of miles from home. No demon could survive the carnage on the borders and glad to see the back of him, the people had begged that a prince blinded in one eye by Arat's thumb take the throne.

"At least I won't have to chase him now," Arat observed. "Burn my castle to the ground; I will not enter it while it carries his stink."

Arat cared nothing for the treasures inside, he always had more and sang heartily from his horse as he heard his brother scream in the high tower as the rising fire summited the stairs and burned his bones.

This was wonderful; the climax of decades of war, but Arat would not have been pleased to die happy, his horse screamed as it stepped on a white hot ember and threw Arat from his saddle. The obese king somersaulted once through the air before landing on his neck.

By the time his death was announced around town, church bells were already singing and children danced round the ruin of his castle. After so much misery, the country rejoiced now that Arat was dead until the homeless started disappearing.

People spoke of Arat's curse, the fact that he was so hated that not even war God's would keep his company and he'd returned to earth as a monster, a blood sucking demon that snatched women and children in the night and devoured them in his lair.

Arat was buried deep with a blade through his heart, but still whispers of his evil resurrection whispered through the town and no mother let their young out of their sight.

"The torch is burning low, we must hurry," Soran sang out, disliking the fact that many dead soldiers had been laid here, expecting to fulfill their duties in the king's next life. Even ghosts had enemies.

Driven by instinct, he reached out for a sword and Richal held him back, not only would the thing be covered in diseases in this stinking pit but Richal hadn't worked so hard to save his brother from starvation to see him impale himself with a sword now.

"I might get enough for a loaf if I sell that down market," Soran moaned.

"I came for gold, not rust."

Naturally there were no guards at the door. The new king was having a hard job making the public feel that kings were something they wished to continue with–it was best to forget or burn Arat's legacy. The crowd would hang him from the nearest tree if they knew he was using taxpayer's money to pay guards to protect the dead tyrants' bones.

Richal and Soran had simply walked into the silent tomb, watched by the black eyes of hungry crows.

"You don't think those stories are true, do you?" Soran asked, feeling his heart rate quicken.

"Don't say that or think like that," Richal said, too quickly. Children spoke of ghosts here, of warped traps created by the obese king himself when he was off his head with too much wine and snorted spices.

Soran looked back toward the door, the moonlight there seemed far away. Of course he hated the dead king too; many of the missing had been friends of his. He darted backward, surprised by a watching spider counting the heads of bluebottle flies in its many webs.

"Brother, we're losing the light."

"I can see fine," Richal lied. Soran was always complaining, in a world as awful as this, the weak died and the strong lived, but Soran still existed through

Richal's actions after so many good had died. Not for the first time, Richal wished he had another sibling, someone strong who would help him through harsh winters and not expect him to do everything.

"Hurry up; I want out of here."

"Stop shouting, you're always shouting at me."

"That's because you're no good," Richal said the truth at last, so close to the gold now that he could taste it. After they split the prize, maybe they could go their separate ways and he wouldn't have to face the shame of having a weakling brother. Maybe he could tell new friends he made in the next city that his brother had been dependable, someone brave and strong. "I'm sick of doing small crimes to keep you fed, I'm sick of killing the homeless for loose change–"

"Y-you did that?"

Richal laughed; a strange echoing ring that had no home in such a place. "What? You think they were just going to hand over their money? I told you, the strong prey on the weak, and I upheld my promise to mom to keep you alive. But now I want my reward–I want the dead kings gold."

Soran remembered the horrified looks on women's faces that had been pulled from the river by the guards. There was madness in the robberies and Soran felt great fear run through him whose source was greater than this place. "God, you're just like him!"

Richal's eyes changed, all remnants of starlight seemed to fade from them, they burned like black fire and Soran had never known that such hatred existed in the world. "Don't you compare me to that tyrant. I am better than him, with his gold I could — "

Soran struck without thinking, the torch caught Richal by the left ear and set fire to his head. He didn't scream as he fell and Soran flinched at the sick cracking sound as his brothers head connected with the ground.

Spiders swarmed toward the fresh kill, jaws snapping hungrily.

"Richal? Richal, I'm so sorry," Soran wept. He had never been alone before and felt a greater sense of dread than he'd ever known before. "Wake up, please awake."

Richal's hair smoldered out and Soran shook his brother roughly by the collar. Suddenly, he didn't care about gold or even making it past winter, he just wanted to get out of here with Richal. He was sorry that he'd struck out in fear, if only Richal awoke, then he promised to do as he was told like all good brothers.

Other sounds were removed from the world when a door opened from the next room, chains rattled and steps lurched. One leg dragged behind the other as if impaired in what had been their previous and wicked life.

Soran said nothing when he heard the labored breathing, the soft hiss of fetid air muffled through bandages stained with the blood of his enemies.

Soran didn't need to read to know the dead king was heading right toward him.

The Evil in the Sarcophagus

DJ Tyrer

The coolness of the tomb came as a relief after the heat of the day outside. Ventriss hummed a tune; Mad Dogs and Englishmen, indeed. The Arabs and Copts they had hired sensibly worked in the cool of the early morning and the evening, but Lord Heston had insisted they were nearly in and had kept the rest of them at it even after the last workman had thrown down his last tool in disgust. But, the lord had been right.

"It's hardly the grandest of tombs," said Jones as they descended the stairs that were behind the hidden door in the gulley wall and, past a pair of cats carved from stone, standing guard either side of an archway, entered the outer chamber, the walls of which appeared to be painted with depictions of daily life.

Ventriss laughed. "We're late to the game. All the best tombs have already been located and opened, their contents removed. At least this one is intact. For all their supposed curses, the ancient Egyptians often looted the tombs themselves, sometimes shortly after they were sealed, more often in times of disorder, while the

Persians, Greeks, Romans and everyone else who have come to Egypt has included looters in their ranks."

"Like us?"

Ventriss looked crossly at Lyons. "Looters don't survey the tomb first."

There appeared to be three rooms in total, although Lord Heston had already set Jones to tapping the walls in search of hidden doors.

"Right," said Ventriss, "Emmett, Rogers, you two start inventorying all the items. Markham, you sketch the layout and anything of particular interest–and don't forget to take measurements." The young man held up his yardstick and grinned. "And, Lyons, make sure you photograph everything. I want good pictures to accompany my report."

"Yessir," he replied with a mock salute. Ventriss dislikes the young man, but he was good with a camera and was already busy starting work.

"So?" asked Lord Heston, generally gesturing at the tomb.

Ventriss turned to the man who had assembled the expedition. As the only qualified Egyptologist, he was the expert for the team. "Well, we have an entrance chamber, then the burial chamber and the treasure room," he said.

"Back there," he indicated the room he had just come from, "is if you like, the biography of the tomb's occupant. Translating the hieroglyphics will take a while, but a cursory look at the paintings would seem to indicate a priest of high rank." Amongst the images of hunting and fishing and farming were ones of cult activities.

"In here," he continued, "we have the sarcophagus that contains his coffin." He indicated the stone structure with a carved and painted lid that doubtless represented its occupant. "And there is the table that served as an altar of sorts and the canopic jars, which hold his heart and viscera.

"Normally, the wall paintings here would depict the weighing of the heart while Ammit waits to devour him should he fail the test, but that's not the case here. These images must represent the specific beliefs of the cult he served. Egypt had a whole host of different gods and a number of competing myth cycles, but the depiction of the afterlife was fairly consistent. Very interesting." He moved to look more closely at one.

"Indeed." Lord Heston's tone was almost as dry as the air in the tomb and returned Ventriss to the topic.

"Indeed. Then, through there," he gestured to the arch that led to the treasure room, "the priest's grave goods–a mixture of his worldly wealth, essential items, cultic artifacts, and food–were placed to await him in the afterlife. Everything he needed to ensure a pleasant and prosperous afterlife.

"Although," he added with a slight smile, "looking at these paintings, you have to wonder how pleasant it might be, wot!"

Unlike the more usual tomb art, that on the walls of the burial chamber was unpleasant; the colors, usually vibrant, were dark and the paintings depicted caverns lit by flickering flames that seemed to dance as he shone his lantern's light across them. In the caverns depicted, multitudes appeared to wail in anguish as they waited to be devoured by what had to be, based on its repeated appearance and its size and prominence, the priest's patron deity. Like Egypt's better-known gods, this one had the shape of a man, but, beyond that, there was little in common with most of its contemporaries.

"It's flabby and hirsute," muttered Ventriss as he studied an image of it. "Possibly connected to Bes, the dwarfish guardian god of good health and good luck."

Had it not been depicted devouring victims by the handful and had there not been something intangibly unpleasant about the way in which it had been drawn, Ventriss might have been tempted to find the strange, sleepy-eyed deity endearing.

"From the ears, I would hazard that it had the head of a bat." He turned away from the depiction. "It's strange."

"What is?" asked the Lord, his tone barely interested.

"Normally, these wall paintings will show any number of gods and goddesses. Osiris, of course, and Anubis, Thoth weighing the heart against the feather of ma'at, perhaps Isis and Horus, and frequently others in depictions of various mythological scenes, but here, the only other deity that is present is cat-headed Bast."

"Hence the guardian cats," Lord Heston interjected.

"Yes. And, possibly, this toad-like creature with the serpentine beard, although that could equally be some sort of demon like Ammit or some other being in their mythology. It's quite unusual." Then, Ventriss nodded over at the sarcophagus and said, "Well, shall we open it?"

The lord held up a crowbar towards him. "Would you like to do the honors, doctor?"

Ventriss took it from him with a nod and called Emmett and Rogers over to help with the lid.

"I don't much like the look of it," said Rogers, nodding at the lid. Normally, they depicted their occupant, but this one had been carved in the bat-eared image of the sleepy-eyed god.

"Perhaps," said Ventriss, "the priest believed his soul would become one with his god in death."

Emmett sniffed. "I wouldn't want to; he's an ugly blighter."

That raised a chuckle as Ventriss rammed the crowbar into the gap beneath the lid and broke the seal, cracking away some ancient putty as he shoved the point in deep. Slowly, he levered the lid up a little way so the other two could get a grip on it and shift it over. There was a peculiar odor as it opened.

Ventriss gave a sudden cry and the lid slid through the startled men's fingers to crash to the floor of the tomb where it snapped cleanly in half.

Lord Heston followed the doctor's gaze into the interior of the sarcophagus and swore when he saw what had startled him.

Where, normally, such a sarcophagus would contain a richly-decorated wooden coffin or, less often, a second sarcophagus of stone, or even, in rare cases, the body without further impediment, this one was filled to the brim with some viscous black liquid like treacle or tar that gave off the strange, musty smell.

"What is that?" gasped Emmett.

"Could it be the, ah, soup produced by a decaying body?" asked Lord Heston. "Perhaps some side effect of the embalming process?"

Ventriss shook his head, although he could venture no opinion of his own.

Jones and the others had entered the chamber from where they had been working, attracted by the noise. Markham dropped his sketchbook in surprise at the peculiar sight, but Lyons kept his head and calmly raised his camera to take a photo. There was a bright flash and it was done.

As if in response to the explosion of light, the water suddenly appeared to bubble or froth.

"What?" Lyons raised his camera again.

There was another flash.

The liquid erupted violently outward and what appeared to be tendrils of blackness lashed towards the photographer, seizing him and pulling him forwards before any of the other men would do anything more than gasp or step back startled and frightened; Ventriss catching something with his foot as he did so. The camera dropped from the man's hands and shattered on the floor.

With a cry, Lyons vanished into the black liquid.

"It's alive!" Jones gasped, pointing stupidly at it.

There was a crash as the thing Ventriss had caught with his foot toppled. He looked down. One of the canopic jars had fallen and shattered–the next one was teetering–and, with a shock, he saw that something viscous and dark had been released from it to pool about his feet.

Ventriss leapt automatically, a reaction born from some primal section of his brain that understood the danger his conscious mind barely comprehended.

Rogers wasn't so lucky. The other three jars each fell over and shattered in turn, spilling their contents, which pooled about his feet–and, then, began to flow up his legs. He screamed, but there was nothing he could do, the liquid covering him and flowing into his throat, silencing his cry. A moment later, he was entirely covered, as if he had transformed into a statue carved from black wax.

In those few seconds, the liquid in the sarcophagus continued to froth and it seemed as if Lyons must be trying to break free from within it. Then, more of the dark, ropy tendrils burst out of it, seizing Jones and Markham, pulling them in after him.

Ventriss shrieked as he felt something seize his shoulder, then realized it was Lord Heston, dragging him into the treasure room.

"Get out of here!" the lord shouted back at Emmett, who was on the other side of the chamber, standing motionless as if stupefied.

He didn't seem to hear and, a moment later, the tendrils shot out for him.

They didn't see what had happened to him. In the treasure room, they were out of sight of the sarcophagus and what it held. Ventriss slumped to the floor, his legs feeling too weak to support him.

"Are we safe?" Lord Heston demanded.

Dr. Ventriss stared up at him in confusion.

He repeated the question and added, "Can it get out of that sarcophagus? Can it follow us in here?"

"I–I–I don't know. How the hell should I know?"

"You're the expert."

"Expert?"

"You're an Egyptologist."

Ventriss gestured towards the neighboring chamber. "I know nothing of... I... " He wasn't quite sure what to say. "It's a monster! It's nothing like anything I've ever read of before."

The lord let out a string of curses. "You must know something. Don't these damn squiggles on the walls tell you anything?"

Ventriss shrugged.

Lord Heston grabbed him by the shoulders and shook him. "Pull yourself together, man! You're the only person who can get us out of here–I can't–so, get up off the ground and work out what we do. Get up!"

Ventriss staggered to his feet and stumbled over to the nearest wall and began to read as best he could in haste.

"I think we might be safe in here," he muttered. "It hasn't followed us."

"That's great for our short-term survival–but, how do we get out past it without being snatched up like the others?"

"Run very fast?" Ventriss didn't look up from the hieroglyphs. "As far as I can tell, this wasn't really a tomb, but more of a temple, a place of sacrifice."

Lord Heston slapped a wall in anger. "And I think we can all guess how they were performed."

Ventriss nodded. "The only dead entombed here were the ones devoured by… that thing. You see, they worshiped that bat-headed god and that… stuff out there, they believed it to be the, ah, emission, or emanation of their god. Thus, by throwing someone to it, it was as if they were feeding them to their god."

"That doesn't help us."

"I'm sorry–are you an expert?"

"Are you?"

"Look, if we can understand something of their worship, perhaps we can find a means to escape. After all, they had to be able to get past it somehow."

"Maybe they just used light; you saw how it reacted to the flash. Maybe we could use fire or something."

"Well, their god seems to be a god of darkness…"

"Maybe there's something in here we can burn. There are boxes… "

"How will you light it?"

"I have a lighter and I would hazard everything in here is dry as dust." He proceeded to smash one of the boxes apart, the silver object it contained rolling away. He broke the wood into strips and bound them into a faggot with his belt. He lit it and it began to burn, but while it glowed and sparked, the light was nothing compared to the lantern he had carried in with them.

Lord Heston swore, defeated, tossed the makeshift torch to the floor where it smoldered and died.

"We might as well shine the lantern on it," he muttered, "for all the good it will do."

There was a sudden sound behind them, soft yet clear, and they both turned.

A figure stood in the archway that led into the next room; a figure as black as tar.

"Rogers?" Ventriss stared at him in horror.

The figure didn't respond.

Then, it took a step towards them.

A sudden thunder crack deafened Ventriss, who clutched his ears; Lord Heston had just fired his pistol at the figure.

The figure seemed unconcerned.

The lord fired again and again, but it just kept coming.

Then, it was staggering backward; Ventriss had shoved the golden head of a staff into its viscous chest and was pushing it backward, using the shaft of the staff to avoid its groping hands.

"Good job!" cried Lord Heston.

But, the black tarry substance had begun to flow onto the shaft from the figure's chest towards the doctor's hands. In desperation, he gave it a push, letting go of the staff as it stumbled back into the other chamber.

"I don't think we've got long," Ventriss gasped, then said, "but, I think I know what to do." He ran back to the hieroglyphs he had been reading.

"It's coming back." Lord Heston fired his last couple of bullets through the archway. "And, the darkness, too!" He swore and retreated, eyes wide with fear, to the far end of the chamber.

"I think they had a sort of rod that could… command it. Look. See?" He pointed at an image. "It is silver and the head of it is like the face of… a toad, I guess."

Lord Heston made a sound like a strangled laugh and looked wildly about.

"Got it!" he cried. It was the object that had rolled from the box he had broken up. He tossed it Ventriss. "Well, use it–command it."

"Fine, fine–let me see… "

"Too late!" The figure that once had been Rogers had entered the chamber, the tide of blackness close behind it, having somehow contrived to move a little like flowing water and a lot like something living creeping across the floor, simultaneously fluid and plastic.

"Right… " Ventriss stepped forward and held the rod before him like a policeman halting traffic. Then, he muttered a series of guttural sounds quite unlike the sounds of the Egyptian language, as he knew them, but which had been painted in a dark stain upon the plastered walls of the chamber.

"It's working!"

First, the strange plastic liquid halted and, then, began to flow in reverse, out of the room. The black-tar figure stumbled in retreat after it.

Ventriss strode forward with a confidence he didn't feel, repeating the pseudo-words again and again like a mantra, hoping the effect would last. Lord Heston followed after him, still wild-eyed with terror.

In the central, sacrificial chamber, the figure retreated to a far corner, while the darkness returned to the sarcophagus that had held it for so many centuries.

"Get out of here," said Ventriss, gesturing to the far archway with his free hand.

The lord ran across the chamber and through the exit while Ventriss stood fast, rod held out and maintaining the chant.

Then, his voice faltered; his mouth was dry.

A tendril of darkness whipped out towards him; the doctor managed to scream the vile sounds once more, halted it as if it had slammed into an invisible wall.

Holding the rod between him and it, he continued to chant as he backed out of the middle chamber and through the outer chamber, before joining his patron outside.

"Dynamite!" he cried, pausing the chant just a moment.

Lord Heston understood and ran to their encampment. Like all such expeditions, they had a supply of explosives to deal with those doors that didn't prove amenable to physical exertion or cunning applications of levers.

Ventriss was flagging by the time the lord returned and was certain the darkness within the stairwell was moving.

With a fizz, a short fuse attached to a four-stick bundle of dynamite came alive at the touch of a match.

His aim practiced bowling at cricket, Lord Heston sent it hurtling into the tomb-temple. A moment later, there was an explosion.

Ventriss stopped chanting, his voice hoarse, hoping the blast had stayed or slain it, while the lord prepared more explosive, which he threw in, producing a cloud of dust and the clatter of falling rubble.

"Treasure be damned," Lord Heston muttered as he placed the remainder of the dynamite around the entrance, he sealed it forever.

Ventriss sank to the ground, all strength having deserted him. A moment later, the lord collapsed beside him, both of them praying the nightmare was over. Slowly, the dust settled and the echo of the explosion died away and nothing moved, save the heaving of their chests as they sobbed with relief.

The Gold Tusks of Ekhaptu

Brandon S. Pilcher

Khalid fished out his curved dagger. Nothing but the moaning of evening breezes haunted the ruins around him. Nor did the waning sunlight reveal even glimpses of creatures stealing about. Nonetheless, he could never afford to lower his guard. He may have ridden further out into the desert than most citizens of al-Khazirah dared tread, but one never knew when one might meet another desperate soul-probing for the same loot as himself. And then there were all the legends of pagan spirits haunting ancient places like this.

Not that Khalid believed such nonsense. Like most respectable Khazirans, he abided by the teachings of the Final Prophet, may the Moon's Grace fall upon him, and gave no credence to heathen superstitions. Those stories were for scaring children and gullible black slaves. The last of the ancient Ekhaptans had retired to their tombs centuries before Khalid's ancestors rode into their region from Aradya. The sands of time would have buried the old gods with them and left only treasures for men like Khalid to scavenge.

Besides, he had a wife and children to keep alive. He couldn't let even spirits scare him away with that much at stake.

Khalid checked on his tethered camel with one last glance. The dagger he held would not have intimidated most rustlers, but a street merchant like him could afford nothing more. Once he sold whatever he found here, maybe he could spend some spare income on a proper scimitar for later adventures. But before then Khalid needed to make do with what he had.

He headed into the maze of ruins. Passing by crumbled mudbrick huts, he picked up articles of discarded jewelry that shone through the dust and shoving them into his robe. He could not possibly collect each and every one of these and still leave room for what he really sought from this place, but stashing away a few extra trinkets never hurt.

A pair of stone colossi sat on opposite sides of an avenue. One had its face eroded away by ages of sandstorms, but the second's had fallen off and rested on the ground facing up. Never before had Khalid seen an Ekhaptan's portrait up so close. Bits of dark brown paint still stained the face, which bore full lips and a wide rounded nose unlike the long hooked ones of Khaziran people. Rows of grooves and notches ran across the left cheek like the ritual scars worn by black tribesmen from the south.

Both statues carried the striped crowns of Ekhaptan rulers, so they must have portrayed royalty rather than slaves like those brought into al-Khazirah's bazaars. Of course, the southern tribes had their chiefs, but none of those could have displayed their paltry power on the scale of a colossus. Nor could any of their subjects have assembled themselves into a settlement larger than a cluster of mud huts, never mind a city like this. Whatever race built the great empire of Ekhaptu, they could not have been black savages!

Khalid brushed away dust from the platform one of the colossi sat upon. Hieroglyphs sandwiched a carved image of an Ekhaptan king holding a group of prisoners by the hair while raising a mace. Very little paint remained on the inscriptions, but Khalid could still make out the subjects' physical features. The king's full lips and snub nose resembled a black man's without mistake, whereas his captives had large hooked noses and loosely curled beards like men of Aradya—like the ancestors of the Khazirans!

More than the cold air of the desert twilight chilled Khalid and made him shudder. A drawing of the Final Prophet himself, may the Moon's Grace fall upon him, could not blaspheme against the natural order of creation any more than this carving. As the scriptures declared, blacks as a race could only be slaves, never masters. This imagery could only be a demon's illusion. Yet when Khalid knelt and prayed to the Moon to set his eyes right, the obscenity did not leave.

He bolted away from the colossi past several more statues along the avenue. All of them bore the same racial features and scraps of dark paint as the first pair. Khalid had hoped the earlier statues represented rare exceptions, perhaps black slaves who had somehow seized power, yet instead they were the norm. Not one Ekhaptan sculpture showed a person of any race other than southern.

The avenue ended before the towering pylon which fronted a temple. Two more great statues guarded the pylon's entryway, but though their bodies were humanoid, they carried the heads of bush elephants. The choice of animal made these images even stranger than any other animal-headed beings. Elephants, always hungry creatures, could never survive in the barren desert surrounding these ruins. The Ekhaptans could have only known of these savanna creatures through trade with the south. Regardless, the sheer height of the temple's pylon knocked the breath out of Khalid. Even if it did not reach quite as high as the grandest Ekhaptn architecture, it would have still dwarfed most mosques in al-Khazirah.

Even though the crescent Moon had begun to rise into the darkening sky, a faint yellow light flickered from inside the temple's entryway. Khalid shivered in his robe again, but at the same time murmured thanks to the Moon for providing him with such luminance. At least he wouldn't have to plunge into total darkness to get what he wanted.

Khalid sneaked through the pylon into a hallway forested with limestone columns. Bright paint still colored in their hieroglyphic inscriptions as revealed by mounted torches that burned as if newly lit. At first Khalid could only hear the torches' crackling and his own sandals' clipping on the tiled floor, but as he advanced down the corridor, a thumping sound echoed between the columns.

It did not come from his pulsing heart. As the beating rose in loudness, it sounded less like heartbeats and more like thunderous drumming. The rattling of sistra joined the drums, and then the voices of men and women chanted in a language Khalid could not understand. He could see no other living figure inside the temple, yet this spectral music filled it as if some heathen liturgy was still taking place within it. Even the torchlight danced to the music over the pictures of dark-skinned people who stared right back at Khalid from the columns. Sweat soaked his face from both the place's interior warmth and his cold fear inside.

He jogged to the end of the hallway, and the drums fell silent. Before him the sculpted likeness of a bull elephant, every bit as enormous as the real animal, rested on its knees inside a niche in the back wall. Both the beast's black granite body and golden tusks glistened with ageless brilliance. Khalid knew an elephant idol had to lie inside this temple, but he had expected something he could carry in his arms. The altar that rested underneath the elephant's head yielded nothing but an empty bowl.

Khalid growled a curse against his luck with tears leaking from his eyes. His family back in al-Khazirah would have slept without him for days now, praying that he would return with something that could fetch them food every night. He could not return to them with only another handful of worn jewelry to sell. He could earn some attention by telling the scholars about his other findings about the Ekhaptan race, but they would either disbelieve him or call for his death. Khalid could not profit from it.

On second thought, that elephant did have some impressive golden tusks. What could fetch better profit at al-Khazirah's bazaars than a couple of big gold tusks? Even the Sultan himself would crave such a trophy.

Khalid strutted up to the statue and sawed his dagger into one of the tusks, forcing all his strength into the hilt as he worked. The blade went through the soft gold with less effort than he expected. Thus, it did not take long before the severed tusk fell off to bang onto the temple floor.

A voice snarled in an alien language not unlike the chanting Khalid had heard earlier. His heart broke out into a throbbing frenzy.

"Who goes there?" Khalid waved his dagger at the shadows between the columns.

The drums rolled again. From behind the columns, a troop of black warriors leaped into the hallway roaring their battle cry. Though elephant masks covered their faces, their white loincloths and gold adornments matched those worn by ancient Ekhaptan men. The soldiers encircled Khalid and thrust their spears' bronze points only a few inches from his neck.

Khalid dropped his dagger and threw his arms up. "No use fighting back. You've caught me."

"So you speak the language of the slaves," one of the Ekhaptan soldiers growled in a language that did roughly resemble Khaziric. "Do you know how we punish such desecration?"

"Forgive me for not knowing your customs, but please have mercy on me." Khalid picked up the gold tusk and knelt at the soldier's feet. "I would have never come here without my family in al-Khazirah depending on me. I seek only something I can sell for their living."

"Thieves always say they have family," another Ekhaptan said. "I say we throw him to the leopards!"

"Restrain your bloodlust, Nekhebu." It was the soft voice of a woman. "This Khalid ibn Najjar speaks the truth."

The warriors drew their spears away from Khalid. They parted their ranks to reveal a slender young woman draped in thin white linen. Dreadlocks ringed with gold framed her obsidian-dark face, which kept an exotic beauty even if rows of dot-like scars ran across her cheeks and brow.

"How did you know I spoke the truth?" Khalid asked. "How do you know my name?"

"Centuries have passed since I lived as flesh and blood in this world, but my spirit can still watch it from the next," the Ekhaptan woman said. "And I have seen many changes to the world I once called home. The summer rains have drifted southward, so the savannas that fed our kingdom's herds have withered away."

"You mean this desert was once savanna?" Khalid shrugged. "That explains the elephant."

"He was Yebu, the god I served as priestess in my time. As our land dried up, so did our empire collapse. Those of us who did not die of thirst or famine fled for greener pastures, such as those to the south. Many of those southern people you regard as savages and slaves carry our blood in their veins."

Guilt gnawed away at Khalid's conscience until it ached. "And this is where our ancestors came in?"

"You rode and settled in our land well after we left it behind, but we Ekhaptans knew of your ancestors in Aradya long before then. In fact, we saw them as barbarians fit for little more than slavery. Already you have seen how our rulers commemorated their victories against your people. Such is the cruel irony of time's passage, for the rulers of one era may become slaves in the next."

"Enough time has been wasted with your history lecture, Priestess Merysankh! Why don't you sentence this jackal's son already?" Nekhebu, the Ekhaptan soldier, banged his spear's butt against the floor. "We must teach his kind never to defile our sacred ground!"

"I will not sentence him," the priestess said. "He comes here seeking wealth to spend on his family, and I would never let them starve. So, Khalid ibn Najjar, you have our permission to leave with the tusk."

Khalid groveled before her feet. "I owe your compassion and generosity more than I can imagine. I cannot leave until I offer one thing in repayment; I shall inform the scholars back in al- Khazirah everything I have learned about your civilization and the black people who built it. They cannot remain shrouded in ignorance forever."

But Merysankh shook her head. "They would have you and everyone you hold dear executed for that," she said. "Someday the truth will come to haunt them, but now is not that time. What matters is that you feed the people you care about."

The priestess and her soldiers faded into nothing, and the torches' light burned away. Only slivers of Moonlight beamed through the temple's windows and cracks in the ceiling. The wind whistled outside, but no other sounds remained. Even Khalid's heartbeat softened down.

Slipping the gold tusk under his belt with his dagger, he jogged out of the temple all the way back to where his camel waited. In the days to come, he would bring not only enough food to feed his family forever but a secret he would share only with them.

Hopefully, for everyone's sake, the children could keep that secret.

The Statue

DJ Tyrer

The Professor was certain he had located a lost city of the Pharaohs. It was his belief that, after a decade of searching, he had found the site of the long-forgotten port-city of Rathesettus buried in the mud and slime of the Nile Delta. That was why we were standing here on the reed-lined banks of a coastal lagoon. He believed that here, beneath the murky waters, lay the ruins of the city he sought.

Legend said the city had vanished in a single night after its inhabitants aroused the wrath of their god. Some scholars argued it had never existed, but most concurred that it had been destroyed by a sudden earthquake. Many of them also agreed it would never be found, but he begged to differ.

I had been Professor Harrington's assistant for three years and had been constantly by his side as his quest progressed from fancy through tedious research to its conclusion here beside an Egyptian lake. Gazing at the brackish waters, one might have assumed we had reached a dead end, but no; the Professor was not going to be so easily defeated!

Soon, he had local laborers working on a network of dams and sluices in order to allow the draining of the lake. Slowly, over the next few days, the waters receded to reveal a viscous muddy bottom that, at first sight, appeared to be devoid of any interest. A closer look, however, revealed the remains of the city for which we had searched so long, concealed in the muck. As the mud was poked and cleared away, the ruins were revealed; the foundations of walls, toppled pillars, and ancient pots were released from their slimy grave.

There was one object in particular that excited the Professor's interest; a great statue entombed in the thick ooze of millennia. When, first, he had a team of laborers pull it from the sucking mud and then drag it along a path of reed mats from the lake bed and to our campsite, it was barely recognizable for what it was; the encrusted mud hid its features and almost totally concealed the humanoid form of the statue. The Professor supposed it was that ancient Egyptian god of the Ptolemaic period the citizens of Rathesettus had worshiped and which was said to have caused their end, although only by removing the grey-brown encrustation would we be able to know for certain.

Given the Professor's excitement about this find, it was soon decided that cleaning the statue would be a priority for the team. Indeed, he even delegated the command of the laborers to myself so that he could begin the task himself, right away.

I, thus, was not present in the camp for much of the next few days, but busy overseeing work at the lakebed. The hands who were in camp, the typical superstitious natives one usually finds in such menial roles, displayed a good deal of perturbation regarding the statue and a good number of them disappeared over the period that it lay there within a large canvas tent.

Checking with Professor Harrington on his progress, and thinking, perhaps, to raise the topic of the camp staff's defections; I was somewhat surprised to discover he had made but little headway in cleaning it off. The statue was still heavily caked with mud and he just sat there in a camp-chair, staring intently at it, a look of deep concentration upon his face. Standing there beside that huge monument, I could well understand the natives' aversion to it–I found myself feeling quite unnerved at its presence.

I tried attracting the Professor's attention, but he did not seem to notice me, so I put a hand on his shoulder and gave him a shake. That caused him to sputter and turn to stare at me in surprise. I explained why I was there and he defensively brushed aside my questions.

As far as he was concerned, there was nothing wrong. As far as I was concerned, well, there was too much work for me to worry about him and his obsession. I should have.

I left him there, his gaze returned to the statue.

More finds came to light, dredged from the mud and I cataloged each in turn. While many were prosaic items such as pots and bowls, there were those that were of more poetic form, such as statuettes and jewelry. Indeed, there were a number of very curious carvings amongst our finds that drew my interest and left me quite perplexed; strange things that looked like frogs with a touch of men about them and beards of serpents. As they fascinated me, they filled me with a sense of unease, a chill feeling akin to fear. It seemed we now had an image of that large statue the Professor was so obsessed with. The Professor still had not progressed far in his cleaning, just continued to stare at it, and was disinclined to accept any assistance with the task.

Perhaps I should have worried more. If I had, maybe the Professor would be alive today. But, I did not and he is not, and none of that can be changed now. He was obviously obsessed with the statue; he had become a haggard and withdrawn man who refused meals and seemed not to sleep. But, it was not any of that which killed him.

One night, a few weeks after we had drained the lake, I was awakened by an extraordinary commotion. I leapt out of my bed, startled by crashes and shouts and cries from outside in the camp. Shadows danced about my tent from flames close by and I tasted smoke on the air. Running out into the chaos, I found the camp a scene of disaster; tents had collapsed or, literally, been torn from their moorings, whilst others were aflame from where overturned lanterns had ignited canvas and crates. A sudden boom shook the night, telling me that our crate of dynamite, held in reserve, had caught light, too.

The remaining workmen were fleeing in complete and utter panic, their cries already beginning to fade as they escaped into the night, abandoning the camp to the conflagration that engulfed it.

There was nothing I could do to save the camp. It was already largely consumed. For a moment, I dithered, thinking I ought to search for the Professor, but a lightning flash and whip-crack bang sent me running as the tent holding our chemicals caught flame.

If the Professor were in a fit state, I reasoned, he would already have fled; if he were incapacitated in some way, then he was likely to already be dead. Either way, I could see no good of my tarrying and so joined the undisciplined exodus into the night.

The next morning, I returned to the smoking ruins of what had been our campsite. Most of the tents had caught light and only a couple appeared unscathed; it seemed my tent was not one of those. I shuddered at the thought of how many of the finds would have cracked or shattered in the heat or during the mad rout.

Of the Professor, there was no sign.

Examining the camp, I had an impression that a horde of enraged elephants had smashed their way through it. Something large, at any rate, which had crushed or thrown aside tents with effortless violence. I tried to avoid thinking too hard on that.

Eventually, I did locate Harrington. His remains were mangled and charred most horribly, making me recoil in disgust. His corpse was wrapped in the burnt remnants of his tent and seemed to have sunk into itself. I had no trouble resisting the urge to unwrap it and examine it more closely. I decided to leave that for the authorities.

Of the statue that had so absorbed his attention in his final days, there was no sign. It was as if it had vanished overnight, despite moving it being a task that would require many laborers over many hours. That was another aspect of the night's events I decided not to think too deeply about. Let the authorities search for it.

As soon as I can, I shall be returning to England...

The Tomb of Necrohotep

Code Name: Intrepid

Robert J. Mendenhall

INTRUDER ALERT
INGOLD AIRSTRIP
April 13, 1935

The man who tumbled from the gondola of the hot air balloon onto the hard pavement of Ingold Airstrip's only runway bled from old wounds. His head and face were caked with dirt made muddy from his own blood. His clothes were tattered, his feet bare. He clawed at the runway with one hand. He pushed with oozing knees and feet, crawling forward inch by agonizing inch.

In his other hand, he clutched a small, canvas-wrapped bundle as if his life depended on it.

A military utility vehicle sped toward the downed balloon, churning a tempest of dust as it cut across the barren field toward the runway. Two men occupied the vehicle, both in military uniform.

The corpulent driver gripped the steering wheel with fingers thick as fine Casa Blanca cigars. The rolled-up sleeves of his khaki shirt strained against the meat of his forearms. His waxed, handlebar mustache lay plastered against his fleshy face and his eyes were somewhere between doughy cheeks and furrowed brow. The circular brim of his campaign hat angled downward, held firm against his bald pate by a leather strap behind his neck.

The driver was Master Sergeant Michael "Hammer" Downe, United States Army.

The second man stood one foot in the passenger seat well, the other on the running board. He gripped the utility vehicle's windshield with one hand and a Smith and Wesson .45 semi-automatic pistol in the other. He wore no head gear, as the driver did, exposing his large and square head to the wind. His wiry hair was cut short and had both the texture and color of clean copper. Eyes large and round, with pupils nearly the same shade of metal as his hair, looked over a squat, pugged nose. His skin was coarse and pock-marked, his teeth uneven and an unpleasant shade of ivory-tan. He was as hefty as Hammer Downe but solid. The hard core of his torso strained against the double-holstered Sam Brown belt. He carried a Thompson submachine gun slung over one shoulder.

The passenger was Gunnery Sergeant Dexter "Guns" Preston, United States Marine Corps.

"There. On the runway," Guns Preston pointed toward the crawling man.

"I see him," Downe said. "He looks hurt."

"Circle around him, Hammer. Better make sure there's no one else hiding in the balloon."

Downe veered away from the crawling man and toward the balloon. He slowed and Preston leapt from the moving vehicle, literally hitting the ground running.

Preston crouched and unslung the Thompson on the move. With both weapons pointed ahead, he approached the grounded gondola.

Downe skidded to a stop several yards ahead of the crawling man. He pulled a .38 blue steel revolver from underneath his seat and trotted toward the crawling man, pistol pointed. The crawling man stopped moving and dropped his head to the pavement.

Preston leered over the lip of the gondola. He winced. Except for a substantial amount of blood and bodily waste, the balloon basket was empty. He rubbed his nose with a back of a hand and pivoted.

"Balloon's empty," he told Downe as he approached.

"He looks dead," Downe said.

As if denying that claim, the man moved his bloody hand and strained to raise his head.

"Who the hell are you?" Preston asked. "And what are you doing here?"

The crawling man pushed himself onto his back. "G-Guns?" he wheezed. "Is t-that you?"

Preston squinted. "How do you know me?"

"It's m-me…Jasper."

"Holy smoke!" Preston bellowed. He slung the Thompson over his shoulder and holstered the .45. Downe slipped the revolver into his waistband. Both men knelt at the crawling man's side.

"Digs?" Downe asked.

"What happened to you?" Preston said.

The crawling man was Professor Reginald "Digs" Jasper, renowned archeologist currently affiliated with New York's American Museum of Natural History. All three men were members of a unique team of adventurers and trouble-shooters attached to the War Department's Office of Special Actions, code name: Intrepid.

"Where's R-Rick? Need t-to see…Rick."

"He's off base with Hawk," Downe said.

"Get him," Digs Jasper said just before he passed out.

ꖀꖀꖀ

At that moment over the Atlantic coast, a barrage of bullets tore through the fuselage of the Consolidated Aircraft XBY-1 Catalina prototype flying boat. The pilot reacted instantly, banking left and diving away from the attack.

"Son of a bitch!" Lieutenant Commander Roger "Sky Hawk" Winchester, United States Navy, swore. His normally perpetual grin now pressed into a tight line under his pencil mustache. His bright emerald eyes squinted behind aviator sunglasses. In profile, Winchester resembled actor Ronald Colman, or possibly Clark Gable. At this moment, his typically lazy features were taut.

"Bogey at two o'clock," the man in the co-pilot's seat said in a rich, even timbre. "It's a Fokker D VII."

If the co-pilot appeared concerned about the strafing, he gave no sign. If anything, his composure seemed unperturbed, even relaxed. This continence often had the effect of calming others in stressful situations and it did so now. Winchester's grip on the yoke eased and his control of the aircraft smoothed.

"Where did it come from, Rick?"

The co-pilot didn't respond. He released his harness and squeezed between the seats toward the stern of the aircraft. Lieutenant Colonel Rick Justice, United States Army Air Corps, was not a small man. His substantial arms and chest strained against the khaki material of his uniform. His face was square with smooth lines at the jaw and cheek bones, and eyes that could have been lenses refracting skylight, they were that blue. He pulled off the khaki flight cap to expose a thick field of wheat-colored hair.

While Sky Hawk Winchester was second in command of Intrepid, Rick Justice was the team leader.

A second volley of bullets tore into the cabin, missing Justice by scant inches. Winchester banked right and climbed. Justice rode the rocking aircraft like a surfboard.

As the Catalina pitched, Justice un-dogged a hatch above his head. The hatch swung inward. A rush of turbulence buffeted the interior. Justice engaged a cranking mechanism causing a Browning air-cooled fifty caliber machine gun to ratchet upward from the Catalina's deck and through the opening in the flying boat's fuselage.

Justice donned thick headphones and high-gauge goggles and climbed through the hatch.

"Set," Justice said evenly.

"Let's go get him," Winchester said. Despite the roar of wind, Justice heard him clearly in the headphones.

Sky Hawk Winchester smiled broadly. Now, in action, his face relaxed and the resemblance to Gable was uncanny. He pulled back on the yoke, trimmed the tail, and goosed the aircraft's twin Pratt and Whitney wing-mounted engines. The bulky craft performed like a dancer under his direction. It pirouetted and shot toward the Fokker head on.

Justice depressed the Browning's trigger. Ribbons of tracer bullets arched toward the approaching bi-plane, clipping the tip of its upper wing. The Fokker barrel-rolled and dropped below the Catalina.

Winchester arched and dove. Despite his expertise as a pilot, the Catalina lacked the agility and responsiveness of the German-made fighter plane. The Fokker came up beneath the Catalina and riddled its wing and starboard engine with bullets.

"Son of a—" Winchester cursed.

Flame and smoke billowed from the stalled engine. The Catalina listed. Winchester compensated.

"Hawk," Justice said smoothly. "Roll it over."

Winchester didn't question the unusual directive. He simply complied, rolling the failing Catalina so the underside was skyward.

Justice had the climbing Fokker in his sights before the astounded pilot knew what was happening. Justice fired and twin streaks of tracer bullets tore into the bi-plane, rupturing its fuel line and igniting the aviation gas. The Fokker exploded in a fireball.

Winchester righted the Catalina, but it shook and yawed as if having a seizure. They were going down.

𓁿 𓁿 𓁿

Rita Marshall eased the door to the infirmary closed, wary to waken the sleeping Jasper. Her auburn hair was disheveled, and locks of it fell errantly across her face. She brushed them back and smoothed her bloody hospital gown. Lean and athletic, Rita Marshall was a valued member of the Intrepid team. Her skills in research, science, mountaineering, and first aid, as well as her unquenchable thirst for adventure, had proven her worth many times over. These were only a few reasons Guns Preston was hopelessly in love with her.

That Rita Marshall was incredibly beautiful, was another.

"How's he doing?" Hammer Downe asked.

"I've cleaned him up and stitched his wounds, but he's lost a lot of blood. He's going to need an infusion and soon. I wish Dr. Lester were here. I'm an okay medic, but I'm not a doctor."

"You're a great medic, Rita," Preston said.

She feigned appreciation with an artificial smile. While she respected Preston as a colleague, his open adulation often annoyed her.

"What about a direct transfusion?"

All eyes turned to the newcomer. He was a gaunt man, pale as flour, with wire-thin charcoal hair that barely covered his skull. The lenses of his glasses were thick as the bottoms of Coca-Cola bottles. Braces clacked as he tottered into the room on polio-ravaged legs.

The bespectacled man was Professor Lucius "Glasses" Wellington, Ph.D., a tenured professor at Princeton University, and another active member of Intrepid.

"I've read about that. But, we would have to find a match to his blood antigen," Rita said. "I don't even know what it is."

"Digs and I have the same type of blood. We're both Group O negative," Wellington said.

"But, Glasses. I'm not trained in that procedure," Rita protested.

"Guns is right, Rita," Wellington said. "You are a great medic and I can walk you through it. We don't have much choice if we want to save him."

Rita nodded and took a deep breath. "Let's get going, then," she said.

Minutes later, blood flowed through thick tubes from Glasses Wellington to Digs Jasper.

♌♌♌

"We're not going to make it, Rick," Sky Hawk Winchester shouted over the roar.

The Catalina was, at most, a dozen feet above the surface of the Atlantic, close enough to see the occasional shark dorsal. Black smoke billowed from the starboard engine, trailing behind them like a comet's tail. The rudder was near useless. The flying boat shuddered and bucked. Winchester's knuckles were bone-white from his iron grip on the yoke.

"Get us as close to shore as you can, Hawk. With luck, the pontoons are intact."

"Aye, aye,"

They could see the coast a few miles away. Despite Winchester's efforts, the Catalina drifted closer and closer to the Atlantic. Inches above the ocean, he gave a heave to the yoke and got the nose up just enough for the pontoons to slice into the water. The craft skipped like a skimming stone, sliced again, then settled. Winchester cut the remaining engine.

The Catalina bobbed on the surface. The tail drooped, but the fuselage itself remained above water.

Winchester leaned back in his padded seat and let out a long breath. He pulled an open pack of Lucky Strikes from his shirt pocket, tapped a short cigarette loose, and slipped one end of the snipe between his lips. He didn't light it.

"Nice landing, Hawk," Justice said.

Winchester picked a loose tobacco leaf from his mouth and grinned. "Any landing we can walk away from, Rick…"

"Looks like the pontoons are intact. We can make the coast on the surface and anchor off shore." Justice donned a set of padded headphones and gripped a hand-held microphone. After he had radioed Ingold Airstrip and arranged for a pick-up, Winchester restarted the remaining engine and set course for shore.

DEADLY ARTIFACT

"R-Rick?" Reginald Jasper leaned forward, grimacing with the effort.

Rick Justice pulled a chair next to the bed and straddled it. "I'm here, Digs," he said.

Color seemed to flow into the archeologist's face. He smiled. "I found it, Rick. I finally found it."

Justice said nothing. The two men stared at each other as if their thoughts were in direct contact. Puzzled by the silence, Downe and Preston exchanged quizzical glances. Winchester and Wellington did the same.

"Found what?" Rita asked.

Jasper told them. "I found The Tomb of Necrohotep."

Wellington took a step back. "Necro…are you certain, Digs? Have you seen it?"

"I haven't seen it, but I brought back evidence of it," Jasper said.

"You mean that stone you had in your hand?" Preston asked.

Jasper nodded. "Where is it?"

"I'll get it," Downe said.

"Tell me about it, Digs," Justice said.

Jasper leaned back and rested his hand on his pillow over his head. He closed his eyes, and when he spoke again, his voice was weak, raspy.

"I've been searching for it for years. Decades. I've chased clue after clue all over the Middle East. I finally found evidence of its location on a tablet I unearthed at a dig in Lower Egypt. But I wasn't the only one looking for the tomb. So were the Nazis."

"The Nazis?" Rita echoed. "Why would those thugs have any interest in some old tomb?"

Jasper went on. "According to ancient Egyptian legend, Necrohotep the First was a priest of an obscure cult that worshiped the dark god Set during the 19th Dynasty. About 1280 to 1210 BC."

"Set?" Preston said. "Never heard of him. Was he like that Greek guy Hercules or somethin'?"

"Hercules was Roman, Guns," Justice explained. "In Greek he was known as Heracles."

"Okay, I still never heard of this Set guy."

"Be quiet, you twit." Rita scolded. "Let Digs tell his story."

Preston feigned a pout.

"Go on, Digs," Justice said.

Jasper took a labored breath. "Set was the brother of the Egyptian god Osiris, and his sworn enemy. While Osiris was worshiped by the Egyptian people as the god of life, including the prosperity of the Nile, Set was reviled. Hated by nearly all. But, there were a few fanatics that worshiped Set in secret. Necrohotep was one of them and perhaps the most powerful priest in the dark religions. Legend has it that Necrohotep made a pact with Set, that in exchange for Set's power, Necrohotep would destroy all of Egypt for Set."

"What for?" Preston asked.

"Because they were absolute opposites. Osiris was worshiped as the god of grain and the god of the Nile. He had been both a man and a god. He was good. He represented light. Set represented darkness and all the evil in the universe. He was the god of the desert and of desolation. It was his nature to hate and defy Osiris, and to destroy everything Osiris represented and everything Osiris cared for.

"So, Set made a bargain with Necrohotep. He would give the priest a portion of his power and immortality, in exchange for Necrohotep using that power to destroy Egypt."

"But, if Set was a god, couldn't he just do that himself?" Rita asked.

"Not with Osiris protecting it," Jasper said. "But Set could distract Osiris, probably in combat, while Necrohotep ravaged the land."

Winchester whistled.

"And so, while Set and Osiris battled, Necrohotep inflicted plagues upon the Egyptian people. Ten of them to be exact."

"Wait," Wellington spoke up. "19th Dynasty. 1200s BC. Digs, are you saying the Old Testament plagues that fell on Egypt were inflicted by Necrohotep…and, not Moses?"

"That's what Egyptian mythology says," Jasper said.

"So what happened?" Rita asked.

"The armies of the Pharaoh Ramses the Second were able to overrun the cult and Ramses' own priests captured and subdued Necrohotep. They dismembered him and mummified his torso."

"So why didn't they just kill him?" Preston asked.

"Because Set had granted Necrohotep a form of immortality. And the ancient Egyptians didn't look at death as we do," Jasper answered. "The afterlife and reincarnation were part of their beliefs. A man, actually a demi-god, as powerful as Necrohotep could will himself back to life, or be conjured back. In order to forestall that, he was ritually decapitated, his limbs removed and scattered, his organs cut out and buried in jars, and then his body was drained of fluids and bound in wrappings."

Preston grunted. "I still don't see the big deal. Why are the goose-steppers so hot for this cut-up mummy?"

"I can answer that," Wellington said, glancing at Jasper, who nodded. "According to the Secret Book of the Dead—"

"The what?" Preston interrupted.

"Shut up, you moron!" Rita scolded.

Wellington continued, "…not to be confused with the standard Book of the Dead, Necrohotep could be revived if his body parts and torso were immersed in a pool of blood and his spirit summoned from the underworld. The Secret Book says Necrohotep would be in the debt of whomsoever revived him and would do his bidding for a hundred years."

"And there is the Nazi connection," Justice said. "It's no secret Hitler searches for occult and supernatural means to further his plans. If the legends are true, and Necrohotep is able to be revived, and Hitler controls him, then the free world is at grave risk."

"Biblical risk, I might say," Wellington said.

"Rick," Sky Hawk Winchester interjected. "Are you actually buying into this fairy tale?"

"It doesn't matter what any of us believe, Hawk," Justice said. "But, in the last several years, Intrepid has gone up against zombies, witches, ogres, a Cyclops, and Norse dwarves. Each and every time the Nazi's have been at the heart of it."

Jasper nodded. "The entire time I was in Egypt, I had the feeling I was being followed. I spotted them at the dig where I found the stone tablet fragment. I didn't know they were Nazis. Not until later."

Hammer Downe strode up to the bed and handed the canvas wrapped package to Jasper.

"Yes," Jasper said, animated. He sat up and took the bundle. "This is it." He handed it to Wellington.

"Blimey," Wellington said as he unwrapped the stone fragment. He pushed his thick glasses onto his forehead and held the object close to his eyes. The stone piece was no bigger than a small book, ragged on two edges as if it had been broken off from a larger object. The smooth edges were ornately carved. The backside was smooth, though slightly pitted; the front side was etched with odd markings.

"What are those queer-looking symbols?" Rita asked.

"A combination of Hieratic script and Hieroglyphics. This is the written language of the ancient Egyptians, dating much farther back than the 19th Dynasty."

"What does it say?" Rita asked.

Jasper took the fragment from Wellington and ran his fingers lightly over the etching. "I've been accumulating pieces like this for years. This is the final one. It gives the exact location of the hidden Tomb of Necrohotep."

"Digs," Justice prompted. "What happened in Egypt?"

"Once I had the fragment, I did my best to stay in public. I took a caravan to Cairo, a bus to Alexandria, an airplane to Malta, then another to Gibraltar, and booked passage on the next liner back to America. I stayed in my cabin for most of the trip. Only went out for meals. A few times I came back and found things out of place as if my cabin had been searched, but I had hidden the fragment. When we docked, I retrieved it and made my way back to the museum, but I spotted them waiting for me there. Five or six of them. They…they chased me. Shouted at me in German. Shot me. I lost them in a…in a carnival. Hid…in a…balloon…" Jasper closed his eyes.

"Rick," Rita said. "He needs to rest."

Justice nodded and they all backed out of the room.

UNDERWAY

The Liberty cleared mooring the next morning with all aboard, including a recuperating Digs Jasper. The food lockers had been stuffed, the supply lockers topped off, and the ammo lockers replenished. Sky Hawk Winchester sat at the controls in the airship's flight compartment, forward of the operations compartment.

The Liberty was not the biggest airship in the world, or even in the United States Navy, which was tasked with the War Department's Rigid Airship program. But she was the fastest for her size. From nose to tail, Liberty measured just over 467 feet with a diameter of over 75 feet. She utilized helium as her lifting gas and could lift upwards of 50,000 pounds. But, like most rigid lighter-than-air craft, Liberty was slow and vulnerable to attack. She could achieve 78 miles per hour maximum speed, with a cruising speed of around 65 mph.

In the gondola's operations compartment, Justice briefed the assembled team on the mission.

"According to the tablets Digs discovered over the years, including the piece he unearthed in Egypt, The Pharaoh ordered Necrohotep's remains to be taken outside of Egypt altogether."

"Why did he do that?" Rita asked.

"Glasses?" Rick motioned to the gaunt professor.

Wellington shuffled a few papers in front of him and pulled out a map. "Because Ramses didn't want to offend Osiris by having a dead follower of Set entombed under the Egyptian sun. Here." He drew a circle with a thick pencil around one of hundreds of tiny peninsulas protruding into the Mediterranean Sea. "Libya. This is where the last stone indicates the tomb was buried."

Justice nodded. "According to the War Department, there's been an increase in German military activity along the Libyan coastline in that general vicinity. But without the last stone, they can't pinpoint the tomb's exact location. Unless they spot us coming in, we should have the element of surprise. I doubt very much the German regulars will attack us, but the Nazi Sonderstaffel is another matter. Once we get halfway across the Atlantic..." Justice leaned over the conference table and unrolled another map. He slid a plastic ruler across its face and traced crossed lines at a point midway between the east coast of the United States and Portugal. "...we'll send out advance scouting patrols. When we get into the Mediterranean region..." he moved the ruler and drew another set of crossed lines past the eastern shore of Spain, "... we'll go under Cloud Cover and ease our way to Libya." He drew a final crossed line over the tiny peninsula.

"And then what?" Hammer Downe asked.

"Then," Justice said. "We find the tomb and destroy it."

"Hot damn," Preston said.

"Libya is approximately 5200 miles from our present location. At cruise speed, we should reach the area in about 80 hours. We'll take turns spotting Hawk at the helm until it's time for scouting patrols. In the meantime, I suggest we get some rest and brush up on our ancient Egyptian mythology."

𓀀 𓀀 𓀀

Sky Hawk Winchester sat at the controls of his modified Boeing F4B fighter, an open cockpit, double-seat bi-plane. Guns Preston strapped into the rearward facing second seat, adjusted the ammunition feed of the tripod mounted Browning machine gun. The bi-plane was attached to a telescoping trapeze by an eye-hook mounted to its upper wing. Even though Liberty had slowed to 45 miles per hour to accommodate the launch, the roar through the open hatch beneath them was thunderous in the airship's hanger.

Justice edged along the narrow gangway between the rigid girder work of the Liberty's interior and the railing surrounding the launch bay. He flashed a thumbs-up to Winchester. Winchester returned the gesture and pulled aviator goggles over his eyes, adjusted his flight cap, and knotted his wool scarf. Preston did the same. Justice moved to the trapeze winch control and pulled a long lever. The winch lowered the bi-plane through the open hatch and into the dawn sky.

Once clear of the Liberty, Winchester primed and then cranked the engine to life. He adjusted the fuel mix until the engine vibrated in a smooth purr. He grabbed the overhead release grip and twisted. The eye-hook snapped open; the F4B dropped in free-fall. When the fighter was about fifty feet beneath the Liberty, Winchester opened the throttle wide. The engine whined and the plane shot forward. Winchester's Clark Gable grin was as bright as the sun peaking over the eastern horizon.

Justice made his way through the Liberty's massive shell and took the circular staircase down to the passenger gondola. He angled through the operations compartment and into the flight compartment, leaving the curtain between the two drawn back. From this position, he could see the nose of the Liberty recede up from view. He could also see miles ahead and miles to his sides. The controls had been locked on an easterly course, so at this point, they only required monitoring.

The team was just into its second day of the three-and-a-half day journey, but already nerves were frayed in the cramped confines of the Liberty. Mostly, the problems were between Rita Marshall and Guns Preston, who could and did bicker under any circumstance.

They had spent most of their time, so far, scanning the skies for enemy aircraft and the seas below for Nazi submarines. Aside from a lone trawler, they had seen nothing. The closer they came to the European continent; however, the greater the likelihood they would encounter some sort of resistance from the Nazi Sonderstaffel—Special Squadron. They would need to be cautious when responding. If a sovereign nation challenged them, they would be diplomatically bound to comply with their direction, should they be in that nation's airspace. They weren't at war and this mission, though authorized by the War Department's Office of Special Actions, was not sanctioned by the United States Government. The Nazi's, on the other hand, were not a sovereign nation, but a political party and the Sonderstaffel was nothing but a secret branch of it.

Sky Hawk Winchester and Guns Preston returned from their reconnaissance with nothing to report except more ocean and sky ahead. Justice and Downe took the next patrol with the same result. On the third patrol, things changed.

Winchester banked starboard as he prepared to return to the Liberty. It was Guns Preston facing rear that saw it. He banged on the fuselage to get Winchester's attention.

"Hawk," he shouted over the rush of wind and motor noise.

Winchester craned his neck to follow Preston's outstretched arm. "I see it," he shouted.

"Looks like a sub. I see men on the conning tower."

"Think it's spotted us?"

The question was answered by staccato cracks and red trails of tracer rounds.

"Holy Smoke!" Preston bellowed.

Winchester banked hard to port and pulled back in the yoke, angling the F4B up and away from the deadly bullets.

Preston charged the Browning.

"Hold off, Guns," Winchester told him. "If that is a legit sub, we don't want to fire on it."

"Legit? It's shootin' at us, Hawk!"

"I'm going to come in low and buzz it. If it's Sonderstaffel, there won't be any markings except a swastika."

Winchester barrel-rolled the fighter and dove for the water. He leveled off sharply mere feet from the surface, so close to the water his prop wash pulled spray behind it.

"Holy smoke!" Preston wiped moisture from his goggles.

Winchester rocketed toward the submarine.

The water in front of him exploded in tiny geysers that sped to meet him as the machine guns on the sub's deck opened up.

He zigged and zagged, using the bullet impacts in the water to gauge where the danger was.

Less than twenty yards from the sub, he yanked hard on the yoke and the bi-plane shot upward in a near vertical climb. The machine guns couldn't pivot steep enough to make the angle, and the volley stopped.

When the F4B was out of range, Winchester leveled off and made a show of fleeing in a direction that would not betray the location of the Liberty.

"That was a pretty big swastika," Preston shouted.

"Yep. No question those Nazi bastards know we're coming."

Safely out of sight of the sub, Winchester made a long arching turn and set course back to the airship.

ℤℤℤ

On the third day into the journey, the tension in the confines of the airship was palpable. Rita and Preston continued to verbally joust with one another, and usually Rita came out on top. Preston, being so in love with Rita, normally didn't mind the attention because, after all, he was getting her attention. But this was the longest and most confining excursion the team had been on together and even his love-struck nerves were getting raw. Wellington retreated to his books. Jasper wrote frantically in his journal, and Downe spent most of his time performing maintenance on the engines. Winchester remained aloof, showing emotion only when he was in the cockpit of his F4B. Only Rick Justice remained unperturbed. He continued to be stoic and focused.

They were fifty miles off the Portugal coast and angling toward Gibraltar when they spotted a trio of fighter planes closing on their position.

All hands gathered in the operations compartment.

Justice unfurled the map of the area and weighted the corners with coffee mugs. He studied the markings he had placed there earlier.

"We're too far out to activate the Cloud Cover. We'll need it once were over the Mediterranean. We're just going to have to fight it out."

"I agree, Rick," Winchester said with a lazy grin.

"Hawk," Justice said, "You and Guns take the F4B. I'll take the Curtis. Hammer, you pilot the Liberty."

"Aye aye," Winchester said.

"Hot damn," Preston said,

"Roger, Colonel," Downe said.

"Hammer, your priority is to keep the Liberty safe. Once we launch, take it to the deck and stay low. We'll draw them away from you.

"Will do."

"Let's move out," Justice said.

Five minutes later, the F4B launched. The Curtis immediately followed. Once they had their aircraft stabilized, they arched under the long frame of the airship and angled toward the approaching fighters. Justice took point; Winchester behind his port wing.

The plan was to get close enough to identify the fighters before firing on them. They were likely either

Spanish Air Force or Nazi Sonderstaffel. They would know soon enough.

The spray of tracer bullets from the lead fighter altered that plan.

Justice immediately broke right. Winchester broke left.

Justice barrel-rolled and set his crosshairs on the trailing fighter, ignoring the lead plane.

Winchester came up from the other side, and zeroed in on the second trailing fighter, also ignoring the lead plane.

Justice pressed the trigger buttons in the grips of his yoke. Thirty caliber rounds spat from the machine guns mounted on the leading edges of both wings. None of his shots hit their mark. The trailing fighter banked out of the line of fire.

Sky Hawk Winchester depressed the trigger on the Browning machine gun mounted to the fuselage ahead of his windshield. The weapon's firing pattern was synchronized with the speed of the F4B's propeller and the Browning's bullets sped through the spinning propeller in perfect time. None of Winchester's shots hit their target, either, and that aircraft banked out of their line of fire.

The lead aircraft rocketed between the two Intrepid planes, the crimson and black Nazi swastika prominent.

Justice dove, rolled, and set his sights on Winchester's target. Winchester followed suit, gunning for the fighter Justice had engaged.

The tactic delayed the Sonderstaffel pilots just long enough. Justice let loose an extended volley in front of his new quarry. The Nazi fighter flew right into the stream of bullets. The barrage shredded the fabric of both wings, splintered the framework, and riddled the engine. Oily smoke billowed from the cowling and the fighter angled down and away. Its propeller stalled. It nosedived.

Justice wasted no time following its progress. The lead aircraft was back and coming up fast on his six.

Winchester's F4B dove and rose like a roller coaster as he pursued the other plane. Each time he had it in his sights, the other aircraft maneuvered clear. Unless he was lucky, this was a stalemate.

Time to change that luck.

Winchester slapped the fuselage to get Preston's attention.

"I'm going to shake things, up," he shouted. "You game, Guns?"

"Locked and loaded, Hawk."

"Then hang on!"

Winchester throttled back and waddled the rudder, feigning trouble. He dipped his wings back and forth erratically and then began a slow, uneven turn. The Sonderstaffel pilot brought his plane up in a long loop, circling over the top of the faltering F4B and completing the loop behind them. As the plane leveled off, Guns Preston, in the rear facing seat, smiled and waved and before the Nazi pilot could comprehend he had been set up, Preston opened up with his Browning.

The Nazi plane exploded in a massive, fuel-driven fireball.

"Hot damn!" Preston shouted.

Winchester grinned and opened the throttle wide.

Justice employed extreme evasive maneuvering to avoid the crosshairs of the pursuing fighter. He recognized it as a Fokker D VII, the same type of plane that had attacked the Catalina days before.

A string of bullets tore through the upper wing of the Curtis.

Justice pulled back in the yoke and jammed the rudder. The Curtis seemed to bounce out of the line of fire.

The F4B came barreling up from below. Winchester fired at the Fokker as they approached it. Preston fired at the Fokker as they passed it.

The Fokker broke to port and dove. The F4B and the Curtis looped back from opposite directions and dove nearly wing tips to wing tips after the Fokker.

They fired simultaneously.

The Fokker exploded.

Both Justice and Winchester peeled off.

As if in a final act of defiance, a flaming chunk of the Fokker's fuselage crashed into the tail of Winchester's F4B, scant inches from Preston. With no rudder or elevator control, the F4B corkscrewed and plummeted to the ocean like a burning meteor.

"Holy smoke!" Preston shouted. "And this time I really mean it!"

"Time to bail," Winchester shouted. He pushed himself up from the cockpit, fighting the growing force of the dive. With a heave, he pushed himself out. The flaming plane raced past him as it fell.

A second later, Preston jumped clear.

They both opened their parachutes at the same moment and watched as their modified Boeing F4B bi-plane crashed into the cold Atlantic.

Winchester's lazy grin waned into a sullen frown.

Justice circled them and when he received thumbs up from them both, wagged his wings and dashed back to the Liberty to prepare for a water rescue.

THE TOMB

The attack of the Nazi Sonderstaffel confirmed not only that Hitler's Special Squadron was involved, but they knew Intrepid was coming. That led to the decision to employ the Cloud Cover ahead of schedule.

The Cloud Cover, it had a technical name, but Cloud Cover seemed more apt, was a complex contraption designed and engineered by Rick Justice himself. The apparatus created an electrically-charged layer of smoke that was vented through the Liberty's outer skin, where it clung to the airship's specially designed covering, giving it the appearance of a thick, cumulus cloud. The color of the smoke could be adjusted from white to gray relative to the electrical charge, and the thickness of the cloud could be altered based on the amount of moisture distilled from the surrounding air. It worked best in high humidity, where moisture was abundant, but the Liberty carried a one thousand gallon water tank to augment the atmosphere in low humidity conditions.

And unless one noticed this particular cloud moved slightly faster than the surrounding ones, and sometimes in the opposite direction, they would go unnoticed.

The Cloud Cover allowed the Liberty to travel and hover virtually unseen. The disadvantage was the airship had to travel at a speed much slower than standard cruise. Otherwise, it would outfly its own cover. This had added nearly half-a-day to the flight.

"Coming up on the target area," Winchester called from the Flight Compartment.

Everyone was gathered around the conference table. Jasper had his leather-bound journal open and was scribbling notes up and down the pages. His wounds were still troubling, but the adrenalin rush he was experiencing seemed to compensate.

"Hawk put the ship at station-keeping and join us back here," Justice said.

"Aye aye."

"No sign of those Nazi bastards," Preston said.

"Or anyone else, for that matter," Rita added. "It's just an empty chunk of rock jutting out into the sea."

"We'll need to keep our guard up," Justice said. "And we'll need to get in and out quickly. The longer we are on the ground, the more likely it is we'll be spotted."

"And lead them right to the tomb," Rita said.

"Yes," Justice agreed.

"Then, let's get going," Jasper thumped his journal shut and wrapped a thick rubber band around it.

"Not all of us, Digs. You're not going."

The silence that followed was profound, broken only the hiss of the Cloud Cover and the whir of the engines.

"I...I beg your pardon?" Jasper said in a low, incredulous exhalation.

"You're not fully recovered from your wounds, Digs. The journey down will be rough. The hike to the tomb will be laborious. And we have no idea what we'll find once we get inside the tomb. The danger—"

"Now just one minute, Colonel Justice." Jasper was on his feet and, where a moment ago he was a bit pale and hunched over, his face was now flushed, his posture erect, and his demeanor defiant. "You of all people know how much this find means to me. I've been searching for it practically my entire adult life. This is the culmination of that search, and I have every right to be down there when the tomb is opened. I'm not one of your soldiers, Rick. I'm a civilian and while I respect your authority as leader of this team, I refuse to follow that directive. If I have to, I'll rappel to the ground on a rope and dig my way into the tomb with a spoon. I've done it before. One way or another, I am going."

Justice watched Digs Jasper with his typical, stoic expression. After a moment, he glanced at Winchester, who made a show of picking a loose tobacco leaf from his mouth. He looked at Wellington, who was busy polishing his thick glasses with the tail of his shirt. He regarded Preston and Downe, both of whom were inspecting opposite corners of the gondola's ceiling. He turned to Rita.

"Don't look at me," Rita said with a wide smile on her face. "You pulled that same act on me for years. It's fun watching someone else give it back to you."

"Colonel," Hammer Downe said. "This means a lot to Digs. I'll watch out for him."

"Have I ever won this argument?" Justice asked.

"Once," Rita said. "Or so you thought."

Justice nodded. "All right then. You all know the plan. Digs, you stay with Hammer."

Jasper beamed. "Absolutely."

"Glasses…"

"I know, Rick. I stay and watch the Liberty. No worries. I'm perfectly comfortable not going toe-to-toe with a demi-god. I'll read your paper, Digs."

Jasper's smiled broadened. "And what a paper it will be."

"All right," Justice said, "Let's move out."

♌ ♌ ♌

Justice edged along the narrow gangway past the empty bay where the F4B had been berthed. The Curtis hung from its trapeze in the next bay.

Ahead of him, strapped into the first single-seat, open cockpit auto-gyro, Hammer Downe was securing an equipment duffle across his lap. His blue steel Smith and Wesson revolver was tight in his hip holster. Another was tucked into his uniform shirt pocket. He gave a two finger salute to Justice as he passed.

Digs Jasper fastened the seat harness of his auto-gyro and winced at an awkward movement of his arm. When he saw Justice approach, he quickly smiled and waved. Justice cocked an eyebrow

In the next auto-gyro, Guns Preston was strapping the two Thompson submachine guns he had grabbed from the weapons locker to the rack at his side. He also wore twin shoulder holsters, each packed with Smith and Wesson .45 caliber semi-automatic pistols. He nodded as Justice passed him.

Rita Marshall was, likewise, securing a Thompson to her auto-gyro. She gave Justice a teasing smirk as he passed.

Sky Hawk Winchester was just climbing into his own autogyro when Justice came up. "Think we'll actually find a live mummy down there, Rick?" he asked.

"Hawk, nothing surprises me anymore."

Once Justice had slipped into his own gyro and secured his submachine gun, he adjusted extra clips and hand grenades in his over-size trouser pockets, and checked the strap on his hip holster. He gave an overhand wave to Wellington at the far side of the shell. Wellington waved back and pulled six levers in sequence. One by one, a hatch opened beneath each auto-gyro. When the doors parted, the gyros swung about like birdhouses hanging in a breeze.

At a second signal from Justice, Wellington pulled more levers in succession and the trapezes securing the auto-gyros lowered through the openings.

Once outside and clear of the airship, they started their overhead rotary wings spinning. As the blades spun faster and faster, the whine progressed into a high-pitched song. All positioned goggles over their eyes and pads atop their ears.

Justice released first and dropped fifty feet before coming to a hover. He cranked up the rear-facing rotary wing and guided the craft a short distance away. One by one, the five others released and hovered.

Justice scanned the horizon. No sign of approaching aircraft. He searched the Mediterranean Sea below them. No sign of surface vessels and no indication of submarines. High above them the Liberty hid, unseen, in an ominous looking cloud.

Justice corkscrewed and angled toward the Libyan peninsula, the others following in a tight formation.

They landed near the area Jasper believed the entrance to the tomb was. The autogyros were concealed, and they began an arduous hike over rocky terrain. Justice led the column and Guns Preston brought up the rear. Twice Digs Jasper lost his footing and went down. Both times Hammer Downe helped him up and, even though burdened with an equipment duffle, supported the archeologist as they progressed. They marched single file for over an hour before finally arriving.

The temperature along the Libyan coast in April averaged 75 degrees. On this day; however, it was well above average. They were all sweat-soaked and exhausted. They broke out field rations and ate a light meal. They reviewed their plan, checked their equipment, double-checked their weapons, and made for the tomb.

"According to the stone," Jasper said, "The entrance to the tomb can only be seen from the seaside of that outcropping." He pointed to a rugged rise ahead of them.

"Holy smoke," Preston said.

"That is a tight squeeze," Winchester said.

"Which explains why no one has ever found the tomb," Jasper said. He started for the rise before anyone else.

It took another hour of hard climbing over sharp and brittle stone before they made it to the seaside. The entrance was no more than a dark, narrow slit between boulders, barely wide enough for a man to squeeze through. They unslung their packs and edged their way through the opening.

The temperature inside the cave was significantly lower than it was in the open air. Rita shivered and hugged her shoulders. Preston stepped forward with his arms open as if offering warmth, but a sharp glare from Rita had him back-step. The air had a strange aroma about it. Not mossy, but an earthy scent nonetheless. It was not unpleasant. They each switched on flashlights and again Justice took the point. They followed a narrow path with a downgrade, leading them deeper and deeper into the cave.

Justice suddenly stopped.

"What is it, Rick?" Rita asked.

"I'm not sure," he said softly. "Everyone douse your lights."

They complied and the cave fell into darkness. But not complete darkness. Ahead of them came an eerie glow. It wavered and licked the walls ahead with strokes of orange and ochre.

"What is that?" Preston asked.

"Stay here," Justice said. "I'll scout ahead."

Before protests could break out, Justice unholstered his .45 and sidled along the cave wall toward the glow.

Voices, low and urgent, wafted from the glow. He crept closer. The glow grew brighter, the wavering more pronounced. A dank, metal odor became more noticeable the closer he came to the glow.

The cave emptied onto a ledge above an enormous cavern. Below, Justice saw men scurrying about. Men dressed in black wool accented in ebony leather. There were no insignia visible on any of the men. No markings of any kind, in fact. But he knew that uniform. Sonderstaffel. The glow came from flaming torches in brass sconces along the cavern walls. A pit had been dug into the stone floor of the cavern, possibly twenty feet long and ten feet wide, and filled with a thick liquid. Two men, one on either side of the pit, stirred the liquid with boat oars. The metal odor was more distinct now that Justice knew where it came from. And what it was.

Blood.

He sensed the others coming up behind him; he knew they wouldn't stay put for long. He turned and held a finger to his lips, then motioned for Jasper. The archeologist side-stepped to the edge and looked over the scene.

"How the blazes did they find this place?" Jasper whispered.

"We'll have to worry about that later," Justice said. "It looks as if they're about to attempt the resurrection."

"Where are they getting the blood?"

Justice pointed to the far end of the cavern. Bodies were arranged along the stone floor, bodies clad in the garb of the local Libyans. All were bloodied and unmoving, but with their arms crossed over their chests in a ritualistic pose. There were scores of them.

Jasper took a breath. "As Glasses would say, 'Blimey.'"

Justice turned back to the others. "Hawk, you and Guns set the charges. The rest of us will look for Necrohotep's remains."

"What about the Nazi's?" Preston asked.

"Avoid them, if possible. We don't know how many of them there are, or how many other passages there are. Shoot if you have to. But try not to."

"Aye aye," Winchester said. "Let's go Guns."

Winchester and Preston took the equipment bag from Downe and slid onto the ledge. Slowly, quietly, they made their way down the sloping ledge to the cavern below. Justice, Downe, Jasper, and Rita ambled down the ledge in the other direction.

They were in deep shadow, making movement slow and difficult. On the other hand, it provided concealment. The closer they came to the stone floor of the cavern; though, the more intense the stench of blood became. Rita brought her hand to her mouth to stifle a gag. The group hugged the cavern wall and inched their way to a narrow passageway, unseen from their previous position on the ledge. Inside, Justice cupped the lens of his flashlight to dim the beam and turned it on. Ahead, two more passageways lit up. He motioned for Downe and Jasper to take one of the passages. Downe nodded and he and Digs Jasper disappeared into darkness. Justice and Rita Marshall slid into the other.

It was a narrow, winding path that eventually circled back to the main cavern. When they peered into the cavern, Rita swore.

Hammer Downe and Digs Jasper stood next the pit of blood, their hands on their heads, surrounded by a squad of Sonderstaffel pointing Luger 9mm pistols at them.

From another passageway, a tall, lean man marched into the cavern. He wore a black uniform similar to the Sonderstaffel, but the leather piping and epaulets were white. His hair was just as white and combed tightly to his oval head, and his complexion, while not the flour-white hue of Glasses Wellington, was nonetheless pale and nearly colorless, broken only by a thin, pink scar across his left cheek. His nose was less a nose as it was a beak. His eyes, in contrast to his face, were as dark as his clothing. Ominous eyes that seemed to radiate ill will. He was not pleasant to look at.

Justice recognized him from a previous encounter. Dieter Weissemann—The White Man.

The White Man strode directly to the two captives.

Justice unslung his machine gun and leaned it against the wall just inside the dark passageway. He motioned for Rita to do the same. Puzzled, she complied. Justice removed an ammo pouch and laid it next to the weapon.

"Well," The White Man said in a thick, eastern German accent. "Intrepid."

Justice slinked from the passageway, crouching low to the ground and hugging the cavern wall, Rita on his heels.

"Tell me, Intrepid men. Where is your leader? Where is Colonel Rick Justice?"

Downe and Jasper said nothing.

Justice and Rita circled the cavern.

"Really, now. This is pointless." Weissemann pulled a Luger from his holster and rested the barrel against the back of Jasper's head. "Colonel Justice," he boomed. "You have to the count of drei to show yourself, or I shall shoot Professor Jasper where he stands."

Justice motioned for Rita to remain. She shook her head in protest, but Justice shot her a look that was uncharacteristically stern. She pouted but nodded.

"Eins," The White Man bellowed.

Justice put distance between himself and Rita Marshall.

"Zwei."

"Wait," Justice called out. He stepped forward.

"Ahh, Rick," Dieter Weissemann said with a wry smile. He holstered his pistol as a second squad of Sonderstaffel converged on Justice.

Justice raised his hands as the Nazi's removed the .45 from his holster and the grenades from his pockets.

The White Man approached and stood a hands length away. He smelled of sauerkraut. "It has been a while, has it not?"

Justice said nothing.

Weissemann fingered the scar along his cheek. His eyes grew darker. He backhanded Justice across his face. A thin gash opened on Justice's cheek; a line of blood trickled from it. Justice eyed The White Man with an impassive stare, showing neither anger nor fear.

Weissemann's droll smile returned. "Bring him to the pit," he told the squad. They prodded the Intrepid leader forward.

"How did you find the tomb," Jasper spoke up.

"Really, Professor Jasper," Weissemann replied. "Do you truly believe there would be only one marker? My team unearthed a codex that predates the stone tablet you found."

"You can't do this, Weissemann," Jasper told him. "You have no idea the power you'll unleash."

"On the contrary, Professor. I do. And the Priest Necrohotep will wield that power at the behest of the Reich and the world will tremble. Did you know that Necrohotep, loosely translated means 'Peace in Death'?"

"Actually," Jasper said, "it accurately translates to 'No Peace in Death.'"

The White Man's smile pressed into a thin line.

Justice caught subtle movement on the ledge and spotted Winchester and Preston. Winchester lifted his Thompson. Justice gave a slight shake of his head. Winchester nodded and the two continued to unroll wire into the passageway they had originally entered.

"If I didn't already have enough blood, I would add yours to the pit," Weissemann said. He turned to Justice. "Where is the rest of your team, Colonel?"

Justice said nothing.

"Come now. Rick. Do you expect me to believe you came all the way across the Atlantic with only two others?

"As you well know, one of our planes crashed into the ocean after a confrontation with a group of yours."

"Ah, yes. I did know that. My condolences. But you seem to be forgetting about Miss Marshall." Weissemann raised his voice. "Bring her."

Justice turned to see Rita, her hands on her head, being escorted to the pit by a pair of burly Sonderstaffel. She gave him a meek shrug.

"Sorry, Rick," she said.

Justice turned back to Weissemann. "What's next?" He paused, then added, "Dieter."

"Next, you get to witness the resurrection, Colonel Justice. Ringside."

NECROHOTEP

The White Man waved to a group of Sonderstaffel coming out of yet another passageway. The first two carried a pair of wooden poles supporting an ornate sarcophagus. Behind them, in single file, followed others, some holding ornamental containers of various sizes, others clutching limestone canopic jars, their lids carved in the image of Set. They marched, goose-step style to the pit. At the very end of the procession came a priest of some sort, clad in a queer robe of black silk, opulent with grand stitching and accouterments. An ebony sash lay over both shoulders, a blazing red swastika on each end. He wore a jet black bishop's miter on his head with a series of swastikas framing the miter like a brim. He clasped a metal-bound book in his hands and held it high over his head as if it were some holy thing.

"Over there," Weissemann motioned for Justice and his team to gather together a few yards away from the pit. The Sonderstaffel prodded them with the barrels of their pistols until the four members of Intrepid were grouped together.

The priest gingerly opened the book to a specific papyrus page and began to read in old Egyptian.

"Is that..." Jasper could barely contain himself, "...is that the Secret Book of the Dead?" He gaped at the book, then at Weissemann. "Is it?"

The White Man smiled. "It is. You've not seen it?"

"No, I haven't. What I wouldn't give to see it. To just hold it."

Weissemann approached Jasper. "What would you give, Professor?"

Jasper said nothing.

"Digs," Downe said. "What are you doing?"

Jasper turned to Weissemann. "I just want to hold it."

"Join me, Professor. And you can read from it."

Jasper inched forward, mesmerized.

"Digs, no!" Rita shouted.

The Sonderstaffel surrounding them parted. Jasper passed the sarcophagus and the containers and the canopic jars and stopped before the priest.

"Don't do this, Digs," Rita pleaded.

Jasper reached for the book. The priest glanced at The White Man. At Weissemann's nod, he held the book out to Jasper.

Jasper touched it.

Caressed it.

Took it.

"Oh, Digs," Rita breathed.

Jasper suddenly whirled and threw the Secret Book of the Dead toward the pit of blood.

In a blur, in a burst of unbelievable speed, The White Man snatched the book in mid-air before it could drop into the blood.

"Damn it," Jasper cursed.

"Too bad, Professor Jasper. But, I never thought for a moment you would turn. And for that lack of vision, you will be the first Necrohotep will kill. It will not be swift."

Jasper was shoved back into the group.

Downe caught him before he could tumble to the stone floor.

"Nice try, Digs," Justice told him.

"You had me worried," Rita said ruefully.

Jasper nodded and lowered his voice. "That book has to go into the blood. The pages are papyrus, which are basically just dried leaves. But, they are thousands of years old. The blood will dissolve the pages in seconds, but more important, if Necrohotep is revived, it is the only thing that will keep him from coming back if we're able to bring this cavern down."

"Understood," Justice said.

The White Man barked orders in German. Fluent in that language, Justice translated.

"Weissemann has directed the pall bearers to submerge the torso into the blood."

The two lead Sonderstaffel lowered the sarcophagus, opened the lid, and removed a torso wrapped in ragged strips of linen, a sight disturbing in and of itself, but made so much more horrific by the total absence of limbs.

And a head.

While the priest read from the Secret Book of the Dead in an ancient Egyptian tongue, the Sonderstaffel immersed the torso into the blood and let it sink to the bottom of the pit. The blood began to pulse and bubble, as if in a low boil.

"Tauchen Sie die Beine" The White Man commanded.

"Immerse the legs," Justice translated.

The appendages that came from the first container were wrapped, as the torso had been, but the linen strips had loosened and hung in tatters around skeletal legs. The legs were immersed in the blood one after the other.

The priest continued to chant, his voice growing louder.

The blood continued to agitate, if anything, with more force.

"Tauchen Sie die Arme."

"Immerse the arms."

Like the legs, the wrapping around the arms were in shreds, the arms, themselves reduced to dry bones. As they went into the pit, the blood became more turbulent. The priest became more frantic in his delivery.

"Tauchen Sie die Organe.

"Immerse the organs."

Each limestone canopic jar was brought to the edge of the pit, its top removed, and the powdery contents poured into the blood. Each time, the pool of blood shimmied with greater intensity. By the time the fourth canopic jar had been emptied into it, the blood was spastic. It's churning was so violent, it splashed well outside the pit.

The White Man gave the final command. "Tauchen Sie den Kopf."

"Immerse the head," Justice said.

The last container was brought forth and opened. The priest's speech was now guttural, his eyes rolled up in their sockets, exposing only white, yet he continued to read as if actually seeing the printed words on the leafy paper.

The thing that they removed from the container was remarkably well preserved, even though clearly rotted with the passage of thousands of years. The head was little more than an exposed skull with patches of flesh and tissue still affixed to it. The eyes were empty sockets, the nasal cavity a dark void, the jaw locked partially open as if in mid-scream.

Two of the Sonderstaffel transported the head to the edge of the pit. There they waited while the priest chanted and wept.

The ground vibrated. The air thickened. The pallbearers lowered the head into the pit. It disappeared below the surface.

The chanting stopped and the blood calmed. The cavern grew quiet.

"That's it?" Downe asked.

"A bit anti-climactic, don't you think?" Rita said.

"Just wait…" Jasper said.

Justice spotted Winchester and Preston angling down the ledge, their sub-machine guns at the ready.

"Wait…" Jasper repeated.

One instant the pit was calm and the blood smooth as a polished ruby. The very next instant it erupted as a geyser might. A bellow, no a roar, tore through the cavern, echoing and thundering against the rocky walls. The Sonderstaffel nearest the pit were drenched with blood. The priest fell backward and split his skull on the stone floor; the Secret Book of the Dead skidded away from the pit. Weissemann had distanced himself from the pit before it exploded.

In the center of the pit, erect and whole, taller and broader than the accumulated parts that had been immersed, stood Necrohotep. Naked and dominant. His dark flesh smooth and glistening in the torch light. Lean. Powerful. Menacing. He was all these things.

His eyes, though, were wide and crazed. They darted back and forth up and down. His fists opened and closed. His chest rose and fell in rapid gasps. A low rumble emanated from his throat. Strange sounds peeled from his mouth.

Jasper said, "He's demanding to know who broke…no, woke him."

The White Man stepped forward and spoke to the risen priest in crisp, ancient Egyptian.

Necrohotep cocked his head in Weissemann's direction but made no other movement.

Jasper translated. "He's telling Necrohotep it was he who woke him in the name of his…his leader? Fuhrer. In the name of Adolf Hitler, the…ruler, I think, of the Third Reich."

Necrohotep grunted syllables of odd sounds.

"Wow, that is really old Egyptian," Jasper said. "I think he is asking why he woke him."

The White Man began a long oratory. Jasper paraphrased. "Weissemann is telling him of Hitler's plan of a world order under his rule. And that by the law of the resurrection, as decreed in the Secret Book, Necrohotep is now beholden to him, I mean to Weissemann, and by extension, Adolf Hitler."

Necrohotep stared at The White Man with those demented eyes. His fists stopped clenching. His breathing smoothed until movement of his chest was barely perceptible. He stepped forward and out of the pit and towered over them.

His next words were clear and articulate.

The White Man turned a shade whiter.

"Oh, shit," Jasper said.

"What did he say, Digs?" Justice asked.

"He said, 'I refuse.'"

"Oh, shit," Rita and Hammer Downe echoed.

Weissemann spoke in hurried, broken Egyptian. Jasper couldn't keep up.

"That Nazi bastard is trying to convince Necrohotep that he has to obey because the book said he had to. Damn, he's babbling now."

It could have been a laugh. It might have been a sneer. Either way, Necrohotep had no more to say to Weissemann. He turned his back to the Nazi and extended his hand toward the rows of dead Libyans at the far end of the cavern.

The corpses shivered and twitched. Several sat up, then fell back. Others jerked to their feet and scraped their way forward toward Necrohotep. He extended his other hand toward the dead men. More rose and hobbled his way.

Distracted by the events unfolding, the Sonderstaffel's attention strayed from the Intrepid captives.

Rick Justice body slammed the nearest Nazi and side kicked the next one.

Hammer Downe swung his meaty fists in rapid pummels, felling three in as many seconds.

Rita Marshall's proficiency in martial arts made her takedowns look elegant.

Digs Jasper kicked the nearest Nazi in the groin and promptly got out of the fight zone. Not that he wasn't a fighter; he'd been in his share of scraps. But he had something else on his mind. The Secret Book of the Dead.

As more Sonderstaffel joined the fight, Necrohotep watched with amusement. Dieter Weissemann, The White Man, disappeared down one of the passageways.

The dead Libyans drew closer.

Downe took several hits that dropped him to one knee. He got back to both feet and resumed swinging. Rita fell under a rifle butt to the back. Her shirt torn, and her face bloody, she swung her legs out in a pivot and swept the assailant to the stone floor, then smashed the heel of her boot on his face. Justice was overrun by no less than five Nazi's, but he remained standing, flipping them over his shoulder as fast as they came at him.

And all the while Necrohotep watched.

The dead Libyans were almost on them when the rat-tat-tat of a Thompson submachine gun tore into them. Sky Hawk Winchester and Guns Preston charged the scene, mowing down the reanimated corpses.

Necrohotep roared. He reached for the remaining corpses and animated them.

Winchester turned and fired into the lifeless mob.

Necrohotep roared again and swung his extended hands to the nearest passageway. A rush of noise, buzzing and clicking and whipping of wings preceded the horde of locusts that burst from the passageway. The locusts swarmed into the cavern and over them all, Sonderstaffel and Intrepid alike.

"Holy Smoke!" Preston bellowed. He swatted and slapped at the locusts.

The insects continued to erupt from the passageway, but their stings were superficial and they fell to the ground minutes later. Necrohotep faltered.

"Rick," Jasper called out. He held the Secret Book of the Dead in his hands. "Necrohotep is still weak." Jasper ducked as a Sonderstaffel swung at him. The archeologist kicked the Nazi in the knee, then clubbed him over the head with the metal binding of the book. "But he's getting stronger."

The trail of locusts petered away.

The Sonderstaffel turned their attention back on Intrepid. It was too close-quarters for gunfire. It was fists and feet. Winchester emptied his clip on the last of the Libyan zombies and dove into the melee.

Jasper scampered to a corner and read the book.

Rita kicked a Nazi to the ground and was pushed to the side. A throng of Sonderstaffel cut her off from Justice and Downe and turned on her. She fought on, but the numbers overwhelmed her. She took a glancing blow to the cheek that dazed her. She took a jab to the head, a punch to her abdomen, a kick to her thigh. Her shirt was ripped at the shoulders and sleeves, the buttons all torn away. She swung on, but the wind had been knocked out of her. Her blows were weakening. She fenced off a swing and prepared to take a hit to her face, but the strike never came. The assailant was suddenly airborne and so was the one next to him.

Guns Preston body slammed a third away from Rita and punched a fourth into unconsciousness. Preston was as bloody and ragged as she was. Back to back now, they continued the fight.

"What...what took you so long, you moron," she managed to say. He couldn't see the slight smile on her face.

Necrohotep regained some strength. He waved his outstretched arms at the mob and roared again. The Sonderstaffel nearest him fell to the ground writhing in pain. Boils burst onto their faces and hands, under their clothing, in their mouths. Agonizing blisters that broke and spewed fluids that burned and formed more boils, again and again.

But the effect and severity diminished by time and distance. Where Intrepid was in the cavern, only Downe was affected and he hardly noticed.

Necrohotep faltered again.

Jasper continued to read the book.

"Intrepid," Justice called out. "Regroup at the ledge."

The team, still fighting, pushed their way toward the back of the cavern. Justice peeled off from the others and sprinted for the passageway where earlier, he concealed his submachine gun and ammo pouch. He scooped them up and returned firing carefully into the throng.

Sonderstaffel were splintering off and fleeing down passageways. The few that remained fighting Intrepid were quickly dispatched. The team ran up the incline to the passage that brought them to the cavern.

Necrohotep bellowed again and this time summoned a river of blood. It raged from a passageway into the cavern, carrying with it a dozen Sonderstaffel that had moments before escaped through that same tunnel. The torrent died quickly, though, and the blood seemed to seep into the stone floor. Necrohotep howled.

"Rick,' Jasper said. "You have to throw the book into the pit." With that, Jasper handed the Secret Book of the Dead to Rick Justice. Justice took aim and heaved the metal-bound book from their position on the ledge. It arched high and dropped with a splash in the pit of blood.

"Nice throw, Rick," Winchester said, his lazy grin broad.

They waited and watched.

Necrohotep still stood. In fact, he looked taller, somehow. Stronger.

"Ahhh, Digs?" Rita intoned.

Necrohotep roared and flesh-eating scarab beetles burst from the stone floor. Hundreds of them. Thousands of them, hundreds of thousands of them.

"Ahhh, Digs?" Preston and Winchester echoed.

"We have to dismember him!" Jasper shouted. "Hurry!"

The scarabs were rising below them and scampering up the ledge.

"Everybody out," Justice ordered. He handed a Thompson to Preston. Justice fired first, aiming at Necrohotep's throat. A prolonged burst took his head off. It fell into the pit. Preston did the same, severing one arm at the shoulder. Justice took out the other arm. Together they tore into his legs at the hip. The torso tumbled into the pit.

But, there was still power in those parts. The scarabs had not disappeared.

Justice and Preston ran as fast as they could in the narrow passage, the clicks of the scarabs shells close behind them.

They leapt through the opening and rolled to the side. Hammer Downe put his weight onto the dynamite plunger. The charges Winchester and Preston had lain detonated. The ground shook and smoke erupted from the opening. The interior of the cavern collapsed in on itself, burying the pit of blood and the priest Necrohotep under hundreds of tons of rock.

They lay still for a long moment, silent and catching their breaths.

Guns Preston was the first to speak. "Holy smoke," he said.

They all broke out laughing. Even Rick Justice managed a chuckle.

Touchstone

Edward Ahern

The black stone outcropping poked out of the ground like a broken thumb. A Mercedes sedan was parked to its left. To its right, an abandoned Hogan waved broken branches toward the sky. Two folding chairs had been set up facing the stone.

Ed Wilson parked behind the Mercedes and watched Felicity jump out of its driver's seat and open up the rear door. An obese and ruddy apparition pushed itself off the seat in stages-Jasper Carbolia. Carbolia spoke before his second foot touched the ground.

"Mr. Wilson. Join me in one of the chairs, please. Felicity, open the wine."

"Hello again, Felicity. Ed, please, Mr. Carbolia. I gather this is the construction site?"

"Yes. You may call me Jasper." The aluminum framing squealed as Carbolia settled into the chair. Ed had the wiry build of an acrobat, and although six inches taller than Carbolia was half his weight. Ed thought of Abbot and Costello. *I'm definitely the straight man here.*

Felicity poured the wine. Her lack of expression reminded Ed of a cat on the prowl.

"I brought the initial plans, Jasper."

"I'll look at them later. I gather you've been able to reconcile the house's design to my requirements?"

"Except for a few issues. But the house could be more efficiently built if we move it forty yards to the right or left, or even if we just blew that rock apart and worked with level ground."

Jasper sputtered wine in his direction. "Never. The Hachunka elders know the stone to be both sacred and deadly. So do I. My house will be the monstrance that contains it. What color is the outcropping, Ed?"

"Black."

"Look more closely. It's reddish black with yellow particles, like the sacred stone inside the Ka'ba in Mecca. Only mine is different. And much bigger. "

"If the Hachunka revere this chunk of rock so much, why'd they sell it to you? Isn't this still their reservation?"

"Yes, well, I induced them to give me ownership to five hundred acres which include the tumulus."

"But why would they give up a sacred site?"

"Money, of course, plus some unpleasant consequences if they didn't."

Ed rose from his chair and stepped toward the rock. "Interesting that nothing seems to grow around it for ten yards…"

"Don't touch it!"

Ed stopped. "I beg your pardon?"

"Never touch the rock. Your instructions require that foundation and building structure will not make contact with it. Comply with that."

"Yes, Jasper. And despite the restriction, it'll be a dream house, on a par with Kubla Khan's pleasure dome."

"Have you read Coleridge's poem? Many think it's just an opium delirium. I know it's a wonderful vision;

'In Xanadu did Kubla Khan
A stately pleasure dome decree
Where Alph, the sacred river ran
Through caverns measureless to man
Down to a sunless sea.'

This monolith perhaps comes from one of those measureless caverns. Such stones convey great power."

Ed pulled Carbolia back from his obsession. "Jasper, I've made notes on the plans where there are still problems with concealed rooms and passageways."

Carbolia's frown cracked his cherubic mask and revealed sullen displeasure. "Tell me about them," he ordered.

The two men reviewed the obstacles. It wasn't a discussion. Ed would point out a problem and Jasper would harshly advise that any problem was an unacceptable failure on Ed's part.

Ed churned with a clotted mixture of anger and fear. *He treats me like a whipping boy. Take it easy, smile. He's my last hope. I can't jump out of the lifeboat because the coxswain belittles me.*

Jasper's face remolded into placidity. "You've seen the site and the tumulus. Improve your plans and meet me tomorrow evening in the restaurant where you're staying."

Ed had more questions but sat in intimidated silence. He opened his mouth again to babble goodbyes and got back into his car. As he made a u-turn, he watched Felicity break down the chairs. Her movements were implausibly fast and limber.

He pulled out from the rutted dirt trail and onto a paved road and noticed a gangly man standing at the intersection as if waiting to see him. He waved, but the Indian held his stare without expression or movement.

The settlement where Ed was staying was just off the reservation. The lighted windows of the one-story motel and diner stared across the road into the woods.

The diner menu focused on fried meat. Ed ignored the taste of the food he downed, then went back to his room and reexamined the plans.

The best woods and steel were useless for what Carbolia needed. He researched online, but all the supply houses offered the same inadequate materials. At two a.m. he surfed onto a screen of the moon's surface. Extraterrestrial. Think like an alien. He investigated materials used in NASA flights and found alloys and plastics that might allow him to shape and suspend the house's clandestine elements.

The house wouldn't merely enclose the rock, it would cocoon it. Its core would be a hidden bee hive penetrated by cantilevered passageways, then gift boxed in squared-off stone and timber. This is beyond eccentric, it's abnormal. Like their approach to me.

Initial business contacts are ritualized-office visit, telephone call, e-mail. But Felicity had approached him on the street.

"Mr. Wilson?" Her words were too precisely phrased as if she overcompensated for lack of practice speaking.

"Mr. Wilson, how do you do? My name is Felicity. I represent a potential client for a house design and construction."

They shook hands. Felicity's fingertips and palm were hardened, like the paw pads of a cat.

"He'd like to meet with you this evening and discuss the project."

Ed studied her. Black hair. Skin slightly darker than the hair. Attractive but deliberately not seductive. Expensively dressed. "I'm sorry. Please tell your employer no thank you."

She remained expressionless. "Mr. Wilson we've vetted you. Your divorce cost you the house and most of your assets. You're heavily in debt from your last project, and your client from that project is suing you. Your reputation is being demolished. We're offering you a way out."

Ed frowned. *Bad news keeps no secrets. What the hell, they'll at least buy dinner.* "Where would we meet?"

Jasper Carbolia waited for him in an opulent restaurant. His skin ballooned well away from muscle and bone. His vest comforted the belly swell but made no effort to suppress it. Ed thought of Sydney Greenstreet, the actor who played oily villains foiling off of Humphrey Bogart.

"Mr. Wilson, your resume is impressive. An undergraduate degree in structural engineering, a stint in the military as an explosive ordnance disposal officer, an architectural degree, several projects that you both designed and built..."

"The last two of which received some harsh criticism."

"True, but projects in which I find redeeming virtues. I'd like you to design and construct a house."

"I don't handle residential projects."

Carbolia's lip tips pushed upwards, but his eyes remained flat.

"This will be 30,000 or 40,000 square feet, with complexities and refinements that I think you'll find will be satisfyingly demanding to accomplish.

"I require a master builder, Mr. Wilson, the sort of man who built tombs for the Pharaohs and cathedrals for medieval archbishops. And a man who must swear to secrecy. The plans will be destroyed on completion of the house. You'll never be able to speak of this project or have it listed among your credits."

In between comments, Carbolia gnawed on a raw steak. "Bleu," he'd demanded. "Just tell the chef to briefly burn the outside and leave the inside cold and blue-colored."

Carbolia resumed. "Mr. Wilson, you'll be well paid for your success, but you'll sign a stringent confidentiality agreement. The agreement penalizes you harshly for indiscretion. I'll assign the work crews for you. You'll focus on embodying my vision."

"But I'm going to need zoning approvals and inspections, subcontractors like electricians…"

"There's no need for approval from the Hachunka and no zoning here. The work crews will have qualified tradesmen. Felicity will be the only inspector on the project and you'll find she is an agonizing task master. She'll also serve as your translator."

"The Hachunka speak English."

"Your work crews will be brought in from offshore."

Ed hesitated. "I'm sorry, but I don't think I can work under these conditions."

"Indeed. I believe the failure of your last projects has left you in considerable debt. Your initial payment, which I have with me, is $150,000. You'll receive an additional $150,000 as each of three construction phases are completed, and $200,000 on final approval. The monies will be placed in escrow so that you have assurance that you will receive it. Felicity, the agreement."

Carbolia pushed aside dishes and glasses to make room for the document.

"Read it carefully Mr. Wilson. Once you sign it, your life isn't going to be your own."

Ed studied the two pages. "My obligations are stringent and your penalties are excessive. Forfeiture of funds received, criminal and civil prosecution..."

"That, Mr. Wilson, would only be the public side of my displeasure. Your rewards will be considerable, but I would exact a painful vengeance for violating this agreement."

Ed knew he should walk away. But, worse than broke, and with no other project in the offing, he'd signed.

And now was waiting for Carbolia in a dilapidated diner. Chipped Formica table top instead of linen table cloth, an almost drained Catsup bottle in place of a cut glass bud vase.

Felicity's arrival stopped the table conversations and started the stares. Jasper Carbolia's appearance immediately afterward reversed the process. No one wanted Jasper to stare back at him.

"I reviewed the plans," Jasper wheezed as he sat down, overflowing the chair seat and back. "Except for the unresolved details, you've been able to capture what I want to do with the house."

Jasper handed the menu back to the waitress with a hundred dollar bill. "We won't be eating. That's for the use of the table and your tip. Felicity, the wine."

Ed explained his solutions and their considerable expense, which Carbolia waved off as insignificant. The two men then discussed equipment and work crews. "They're Haitian," Jasper allowed, "I find they give Felicity and me the proper respect. They speak almost no English, but Felicity can translate from the Creole for you.

"You'll be quartered on site in a tent. You won't be able to leave and will have to surrender all your electronic devices. Your computerized applications will be handled by a terminal that Felicity will oversee. Complete isolation and secrecy. I'm sorry for any inconvenience."   But his hard smile showed no sympathy.

After Jasper and Felicity's procession out of the restaurant, Ed ordered and ate. *Carbolia's insane and Felicity's a barely restrained attack dog. But I took his money, God help me. If it stays a secret, maybe nobody would know if it turns out badly.*

Ed had walked back to the door of his motel room when he was grabbed by the arm. It was the same Indian he'd seen near the construction site.

"Mr. Wilson."

"Jesus, you scared me. You move pretty quietly."

"Must be the genes. Don't do it, Mr. Wilson."

"Do what."

"Whatever Carbolia is asking. He's vicious. We should know."

"What's your name?"

"John."

"Let's get out of the open, John, and into my room. We need to talk."

John refused the offer of a drink and began without prompting. "Carbolia approached our tribal elders last year. He offered us a half million dollars for 500 acres of scrub forest worth maybe $200 an acre. But it included our most sacred place, and after some arguing among ourselves we turned him down.

"Then he showed us the debt he'd bought up. All our debt-cars, trailers, mortgages, appliances, personal loans. A lot of it was past due. He'd forgive all the loans if we agreed to sell. We're used to being in bad debt and told him to fuck off. Then he told us about our outstanding warrants and the crimes and drug dealing he knew about. If we refused, he gives the cops the whole list and makes sure we're prosecuted. We caved in and sold. Now we have to sneak back onto our own land."

"But why come to me? I can't help you."

"We need to know what he's going to do with the rock, and stop him if we have to."

"Nothing I know of. Once the project is completed and he moves in I can't say. Why's this rock so important, John?"

"The elders say the stone is deadly and never let us touch it. They say it offers great power but eats you inside-out, like a tapeworm. Carbolia wants the rock very badly, so he must think he can control it."

Suspicions confirmed. I'm working for a madman. "I think we need to help each other, John."

They talked for another hour. After John left Ed reopened the plans and began to make notations on a separate sheet of paper.

The first work crew arrived the following week, along with the excavating equipment. The Haitians took their orders through Felicity and avoided contact with Ed. Their timid glances at her showed their fear. In the evening, the Creole lilts coming from their campground were subdued with anxiety.

Felicity treated the crew as disposables. Ed once came upon her beating a worker with a section of two by four. The worker never fought back, or even screamed. When Ed stepped in to try and stop the beating she glared at him with the wordless assurance that he would be included in the beating if he interfered. He ashamedly backed off.

Felicity also lived on site, but occasionally left on errands for Carbolia. As the weeks passed Ed found himself attracted to her despite his fear, but knew she needed to be treated like a dangerous exotic-achingly pretty but best kept behind reinforced glass.

One evening when Felicity was away a worker who spoke a little English snuck up to Ed.

"Monsieur?"

"Yes. René, isn't it?"

"Oui. Monsieur I need to ask you something. Could you contact my wife, Claudia? She is enceinte-pregnant. Please tell her the work is going well and ask how she is..."

"But I have no way to contact her, René."

René persisted pushing a scrap of paper with a telephone number into Ed's hand. "When you have a chance, Monsieur." And he slipped back into the dusk.

No way in hell am I going to risk calling this woman. If Felicity finds out about the stashed satellite phone, I'm cooked.

The footings went in, the foundation was poured. The framing went up quickly. The weather stayed unusually dry, letting them jump ahead of schedule. The first work crew was shipped out and a second crew brought in. Carpenters and stonemasons and electricians. They were equally fearful.

Ed's pride in the design and construction swelled. *God help me, I'm becoming an emotional hostage to this house. But I need to know a lot more about what Carbolia and Felicity are up to. Now that René is back in Haiti he might be willing to talk.* He risked a satellite call. "Hello. Claudia La Pierre? Yes, I'd like to speak with René, please."

The woman shrieked. "René never return Monsieur. The entire crew is missing. What do you know of my René?"

"Ah, nothing. Just that he was to be paid and sent back."

"The money, yes, the money arrived, but René and the others never. Where are you calling from? Where was he working? I must tell the police!"

Ed hung up. *Were they killed to protect the house's secrets? No one knows the secrets better than I do.* He called John.

"Did you get all the supplies we talked about?"

"We had to steal some of it, but yes I've got them. I'll drop them where I told you. Remember-you can do whatever you like to the house, but the stone can't be harmed."

The house gestated, skin of stone, muscles of pressure treated woods, inside linings of wonderfully carved mahogany, Italian tiles, and finely woven middle-eastern tapestries and curtains. Its vast rooms resonated without echo. The labor pains would give birth to a mansion in which Ed took a father's pride.

The secrets chambers of the house also took form. Cunningly hidden accesses led to rooms within the inner hive. The monolith itself was approached through a concealed passageway bristling with man traps. A final walkway of raw ash planks lead just up to the outcrop.

Ed devoted the nights of Felicity's occasional absences to crafting the material John had smuggled in for him. The night of her last absence he spent with the stone. In the hissing lantern light, the outcropping's blacks and reds and yellows seemed to swirl, delivering multi-colored dust for Ed to breathe. As the work progressed, Ed developed a palsy. At one point, he blacked out and woke up vomiting blood.

That next morning Ed felt fatalistically powerful. A berserker must feel like this. Felicity returned and immediately sensed a change in him. Her guarded posture said she no longer treated him as easy prey.

One post-midnight she slunk into his tent and slid onto his cot.

"Felicity, what, uh. I'm not sure this is a good idea."

She said nothing, just began removing clothes.

"Carbolia won't like this. Especially if he thinks you're the Abyssinian maid, Coleridge talks about in his poem."

Felicity began removing his clothing. They coupled without words, an urgent, affectionless ritual that somehow sanctified Ed's transformation. He woke briefly to observe Felicity searching his tent. She left before morning.

The furnishings for the house began arriving, a collection of museum quality furniture, carpets, lamps and oil paintings. So far as Ed could tell, all of it had been created well before the First World War.

The last work crew left, cheerfully unaware that the crews which preceded them had vanished.

Carbolia arrived the day after the last picture had been hung. The service lines into the house had been buried, the remains of the Hogan long since torn down and burnt. The house stood alone, its clean lines shrugging off the surrounding scrub trees like a bad joke. Carbolia sat alone in a folding chair and admired the façade.

"Let's go in," he finally ordered. The procession into the temple was slow, Carbolia hampered by his weight and a desire to exact maximum enjoyment from his visit. The rooms were grand, furnished in that cluttered Victorian style that pulls the eye from one unique piece to another as if the rooms were stocked to infinity with objets d'art.

"Let's see the monolith." The booby traps were not yet activated, and Ed explained them one by one as they moved into the bowels of the house. Ed and Felicity hung back when they reached the ash planking and Carbolia lumbered forward on his own. The inner sanctum was lit by animal fat candles and not electricity. He leaned forward at the end of the planking and breathed on the outcrop as if infusing himself into it.

Abruptly he turned back. "Odd, I thought it would feel different. But well done, Mr. Wilson, very well done. You're indeed a master builder. Let's go back and make a toast."

They sat in overstuffed leather chairs and looked out over alder and birch thickets. Felicity gave them each a glass of wine and then stood at Ed's side.

"Ed, you've crafted my jewel case excellently and are to be congratulated. It's a masterpiece. But I'm afraid that I have to welsh on part of our agreement."

"You've already paid me, Jasper."

"Um. I've told you about my need for absolute secrecy. That, unfortunately, includes you." Carbolia's cherubic face crinkled into a gargoyle mask. "Felicity will be killing you shortly."

Ed glanced at Felicity, poised and expressionless beside him. His own forced politeness sloughed off, leaving bony edges. "Jasper, I've signed your agreement and kept to it. Let me just walk away."

"I can't my boy. We have to ensure the greater-I was about to say good, but that wouldn't be appropriate, would it? The greater potential. Don't take it personally."

Ed's smile glinted. "I'm not so sure Felicity will be able to do as you order, Jasper, I took out some insurance. Look out the window into the alders on your left."

Carbolia's massive head bobbled left as Ed took a small remote from his shirt pocket. He keyed the remote and a half-dozen alders exploded into the air, shredded and torn. The roar of the blast rattled the glasses on their side tables.

Carbolia quivered in his chair. Felicity, Ed noted, hadn't moved at all, still focused on him.

"I suspected that you'd want me disposed of. Do you remember my resume? Bomb disarmers are also good at rigging up bombs. I've planted thoroughly booby trapped charges adjacent to the rock. So long as I continue to send a coded message the rock survives."

"You're an idiot. Felicity will just torture you until you tell us how to disarm it."

"Now who's being the idiot? You'd kill me in any case, but you wouldn't know if I'd told you the truth until it was too late."

"The rock will survive a little concussion."

"I think not. It's deeply veined and fissured. A blast of any size turns it into rubble. But it's just term insurance. In two years it deactivates. By then you should be reasonably confident I won't talk."

Carbolia's fingers clenched. "It's an impossible situation, Mr. Wilson. I can't risk the monolith and I can't risk your talking. Felicity…"

Her eyes shifted to Carbolia while holding Ed in her peripheral vision.

"Take away Mr. Wilson's remote and then cut the power to the house."

"Bad move," Ed interjected quickly. "You may know black stones, but I know explosive devices. Here Felicity, take the remote. It's not the triggering device you need. The dead man switch is safe elsewhere. I borrowed some tricks from Second World War German ordinance. The device is antimagnetic, anti-light, and extremely sensitive to sound and disturbance. Plus a few refinements of my own.

"Let me go, Carbolia. I can't say a word about this place without getting into serious trouble. Fair is fair. I followed the terms of the agreement. I'm paid up and won't be asking for anymore."

Carbolia's porcelain-doll face roiled and then recovered. "Well, sir. You appear to have the upper hand for now. But you should know that I'm an extremely patient man, given to thoroughly thinking through my problems. Felicity, give Mr. Wilson back his electronic devices and take him to his car. Au Revoir, Mr. Wilson."

Felicity was deferential as she drove. "You've gained power," she concluded, "and lost your cowardice. And become something else." She dropped him at his car. "You may have use for me later."

Two hundred miles down the road he called John a last time.

"It over, John."

"The rock is safe? You're safe?"

"Carbolia won't be damaging the stone, nor misusing it."

"How can you be sure?

"It's too precious to him to damage, and I'm pretty sure the stone won't do what he wants it to."

"So you believe now that the stone has power?"

"Yes, unfortunately. Your elders were right, no good comes of touching that stone. Thanks again for your help."

Ed resumed driving. He'd broken his word to John and Carbolia on the same promise-that he wouldn't damage the stone. But he'd drilled a hole in its side to plant the explosives.

And as he'd stuffed in the plastique the stone had enveloped his arm, taking him like a thirteen-year-old virgin and filling him with a burning elixir. It smoldered in him now. Felicity had sensed it. He was gaining fearful power but watching what he had been burn away.

The last lines of Coleridge's poem came back to him,

'And all should cry, Beware! Beware!
His flashing eyes, his floating hair
Weave a circle round him thrice
And close your eyes with holy dread,
For he on honey-dew hath fed
And drunk the milk of Paradise.'

Contributors

Edward Ahern

Ed resumed writing after forty odd years in foreign intelligence and international sales. He has his original wife, but advises that after forty-five years, they are both out of warranty.

Ed has had forty-seven stories published thus far. He dissipates his free time in German, French and Japanese language groups, fly fishing and shooting.

Rekha Ambardar

Rekha has published over one hundred genre and mainstream stories in print and electronic magazines. She is the author of two romance novels.

E.W. Farnsworth

E.W. Farnsworth lives and writes in Arizona. Fifty of E.W. Farnsworth's short stories has been published in 2015. His collected western stories and spy stories also appeared in 2015. Two novels, John Fulghum Mysteries and Engaging Rachel, both from Zimbell House Publishing, will be released in December 2015. Bitcoin Fandango, his mystery/thriller about combating Bitcoin crimes, appeared in March, 2015. See www.ewfarnsworth.com to follow his works.

Stephen McQuiggan

Stephen is proof of Intelligent Design; evolution could never explain how this useless lump of slobber and gristle still manages to draw breath, or what function it could possibly serve. His first novel, A Pig's View of Heaven, is available now from Grinning Skull Press.

Robert J. Mendenhall

Robert is a retired police officer, retired Air National Guardsman, and a former Broadcast Journalist for the American Forces Network, Europe.

An active member of Science Fiction and Fantasy Writers of America, he writes in multiple genres including science fiction, crime and suspense, and horror.

Visit his website at www.robertjmendenhall.com or follow him on Twitter @RobtJMendenhall. He lives outside Chicago with his wife and fellow writer, Claire. And many animals.

Brandon S. Pilcher

Brandon has a B.A. in Biological Anthropology from the University of California in San Diego, CA, and is currently studying computer game design at Coleman University in the same city.

He enjoys drawing and writing fantasy and historical fiction in his spare time.

DJ Tyrer

DJ is the person behind Atlantean Publishing and has been widely published in anthologies and magazines in the UK, the USA and elsewhere, including A Grimoire of Eldritch Inquests, Volume I (Emby Press), State of Horror: Illinois (Charon Coin Press), Steampunk Cthulhu (Chaosium), Tales of the Dark Arts (Hazardous Press), Ill-considered Expeditions (April Moon Books), Sorcery & Sanctity: A Homage to Arthur Machen (Hieroglyphics Press), and Mysteries of Suspense, The Steam Chronicles, Pagan and Tales from the Grave (Zimbell House), and in addition, has a novella available in paperback and on Kindle, The Yellow House (Dunhams Manor).

You can follow DJ on his website at: http://djtyrer.blogspot.co.uk/

Matthew Wilson

Matthew has had over 150 appearances in such places as Horror Zine, Star*Line, Spellbound, Illumen, Apokrupha Press, Hazardous Press, Gaslight Press, Sorcerers Signal, Zimbell House Publishing and many more.

He is currently editing his first novel.

Additional Anthologies from Zimbell House Publishing

Reflections: Michigan 2015
Reflections: Seasons 2015
The Fairy Tale Whisperer
Puppy Love: 2015
The Mysteries of Suspense
Garden of the Goddesses
Elemental Foundations
Romantic Morsels
The Steam Chronicles
Pagan
Tales from the Grave
The Adventures of Pirates

Coming Soon from Zimbell House Publishing

Travelers
Dark Monsters
On a Dark and Snowy Night
Where Cowboys Roam
The Key

www.ingramcontent.com/pod-product-compliance
Lightning Source LLC
Chambersburg PA
CBHW051759050726
47598CB00006B/2356